PRESCRIPTION FOR DANGER

PRESCRIPTION FOR DANGER

A Novel of the Old West

by

Ardath Mayhar

Writing as "Frank Cannon"

The Borgo Press
An Imprint of Wildside Press

MMVII

SECOND EDITION

CONTENTS

FOREWORD

When I first began writing westerns, I was determined to avoid as many *clichés* of the genre as I could manage. First of all, I knew that families were extremely important to everyone, no matter what the historical era involved, and writing a western story without taking into consideration the effects of the plots on the families involved was illogical.

Then I knew from family history, as well as a wide reading in journals and other contemporary records, that the women who went west were not the wimpy or whorish sorts depicted in all too many novels and movies. I wanted to show real people dealing inventively and bravely with unusual and interesting challenges. In each of these three books I feel that I may, to some extent, have succeeded in reaching some of those goals.

—Ardath Mayhar (Frank Cannon)
Chireno, Texas
September 2006

CHAPTER ONE

The train rattled and swayed along its raw road-bed between tall cliffs of pine and oak and sweet gum. Nicholas Blasingame shifted his weight on the uncomfortable seat and pondered on his latest undertaking...then he caught himself. That was a poor choice of words for a physician at any time. One who has been accused of malpractice and practically run out of his own city would do well to avoid such terms, even in thinking to himself.

He gazed out at the sodden greenery of the tree-scape moving past the streaked window. He had asked the ticket seller the meaning of the letters HE&WT that marked the boxcars attached behind the passenger car. The man had grinned, spat a slug of tobacco juice neatly into a shiny spittoon, and drawled, "We call it Hell, Enny Way you Take it." Now Nicholas understood why.

Turning his gaze away from the unbroken and monotonous forest, he found himself staring at a man who sat three rows down and across the aisle from him. There were others in the car, but he found himself uninterested in drummers and portly businessmen. Only this one man, in beautifully cut English tweeds, caught at his imagination.

Though he could see only the back of his head and the angle of a cheek, he thought that one must be rather arrogant than otherwise. This head was held with an air that Nicholas recognized. It wasn't at all uncommon in Baltimore, but it stood out oddly here in the wilds of East Texas.

There was a gust of cold dampness as someone opened the door at the end of the car. Blasingame turned in time to see a burly character in nondescript woolens lurch into the car. The moving air brought a strong reek of rotgut with it, as the man looked about groggily and decided on a seat. Nicholas thought he must have been standing on the platform with his bottle ever since the train left San Pablo an hour ago.

As the doctor looked back toward the front of the car, his eyes caught those of the man in tweeds. The face came as a shock. Though it held the long-skulled British breeding that he'd expected from the man's demeanor, it quite literally held nothing else.

The chilly eyes were blank as a steel plate. The smooth-shaven cheeks and chin were without a line or curve to denote any feeling, even of interest. If a dark blond moustache hadn't given the eye something on which to rest. Nick felt his gaze might have slid right down to the lean but muscular shoulders, whether he wanted it to or not. What was more disturbing was the fact that those still eyes held something like recognition. That was a thing Blasingame could do without at this point. He was still too sore over the outcome of his ill-fated crusade against the unhealthful conditions he'd found in his cousin's rental properties. The horrified realization that neither kinship nor his own spotless record could save him from being crucified by the political machine raking in wealth from the landlords it was protecting had not yet healed.

Hiram Connaughty's death at the age of eighty-seven from emergency surgery on a perforated ulcer had given the ugly crew at City Hall exactly the lever they had needed. With it they had pried Nicholas Blasingame out of their hair.

He wrenched his gaze away. He hoped that the well-dressed person down the car was going a lot farther than he himself intended to go. He settled back into an uncomfortable corner and took his cousin Alicia's letter from his breast pocket. Bless Alicia!

She had been more like a sister than a cousin. While the family had been aghast when she decided to go with her fiddle-footed husband into the Terra Incognita of Texas, he had wished her well, even though he hated to lose her steady good sense and warm loyalty. And now she had come to his rescue.

She had written:

> Moreno has now some five thousand people, with more coming all the time since the completion of the railroad. There is no doctor nearer than San Pablo, a day's ride away. With the work now going on at the iron mine nearby, there is much need for medical care beyond that now available. Injuries are almost a daily occurrence, along with snakebite, fist-fights, gun-fights, childbirth, and incidental illness.
>
> Though the town does have its _problems_ [she had underlined the word heavily], you have had enough experi-

ence, now, at fighting City Hall to know how to avoid confrontations. Heaven knows, there will be more than you can possibly do as a doctor.

Bartholomew is fairly well placed here. We have opened a general store, which is doing very well, what with newcomers arriving to work at the mine. There is also a lot of activity in land speculation as well as timber, which grows here to incredible size and very quickly.

All in all, I believe that you will find the setting so different, the work so engrossing, and the citizenry so unlike that of Baltimore that you will, in time, feel free of the bitterness that rang all through your last letter. Come, dear Nick, and try us out at least. I cannot believe that you want to go directly back into the sort of situation you left in Baltimore, which is common all through the East.

He had thought long and hard before leaving his native Maryland. His family had been there since before the Revolution, and his roots went deep, without his realizing the fact. Still, he had found himself stifling in the cynical atmosphere that was permeating business and government and even medicine. Now he was clattering along toward Moreno, the town with "problems," where Alicia and Bart waited for him.

His eyes once more turned toward the forest that

seemed to be an endless part of this new country. He could see, even as the train moved, that the pines were, indeed, huge, though they were mixed with thick stands of hardwood laced with vine, so that only the crowns stood stiffly against the slow rainfall. As he watched, the cloud thickened into darkness almost as dense as night. Behind him, someone lit the lamps.

His own face, too thin, a bit haggard, gazed back like a ghost, mirrored against the background darkness in the dirty glass. He shivered. Something inside him tingled...almost like a warning.

They pulled into Moreno after dark. Lanterns swung from the jerry-built depot porch. A dozen or more people milled between the track and the train, so that it was an anxious several minutes before he saw Alicia's fair head glint under one of the lights.

He waved and called. Miraculously, she heard him above the hubbub. She raised a gloved hand and waved, pointing toward his left. There he saw Bart shouldering his way among the throng toward the passenger car. Nicholas bundled his scanty baggage together and stepped down to meet his cousin-in-law. Bart looked older, more settled somehow, than he ever had in Baltimore. He carried himself with an assurance that Nick would never have believed five years ago when he and Alicia had said goodbye. Nick saw with some unease that Bart carried a pistol in his coat pocket, as the younger man reached down to lift one of his bags.

"Nick!" said Bart. His voice was stronger and quieter than it used to be. "Glad you could come. We need a doctor so badly...well, you will see. Come over and say hello to Al. She's been on pins and needles ever since she got your note."

"I'm grateful that you asked me," Blasingame said, thrusting his way through the crowd in order to follow Bart. He bumped into someone and said an automatic, "Pardon me," before he realized that it was the man from the train.

They stood for an instant—not more than that—regarding one another; then the stranger nodded and turned away, leaving Nick to struggle on toward Alicia, who was beaming at him with all the good will in the world.

After an enthusiastic hug, he stepped back and looked her over. Gone was the frail girl he had known for so many years. She was now lightly tanned, even this early in the spring, and her shoulders and arms had filled out with sound flesh and muscle. A flush of health underlay her skin, and the blue veins that had worried him for years were now invisible.

Except for a line between her brows, her face was untroubled. Blooming, in fact. He turned to Bart and shook his hand. "Now I know why this girl wanted me to come! When is the baby due?"

Alicia laughed and tucked her hand in the crook of his elbow. "I wasn't even pregnant when I wrote you. And the child isn't due for another seven months. Nobody but a doctor would have known...at least, nobody here does, except for the two of us and Carry-Ann. But don't doubt that I'm more than glad to have you here, and not only for that single reason."

She smiled. "Now come and have supper. You must be famished." She stepped away, turning, and a raw-boned man who had been watching them

14

closely took the opportunity to speak to her.

"Evening, Bart. Miz Hazelton. Got company eh? Kinfolks?" His black eyes held no warmth, and his tone was barely civil, though Nick could find nothing wrong with the words.

Alicia drew back, as if his touch might contaminate her gray skirts. She looked him full in the eyes and said, "Sheriff Tolliver, I would like you to meet my cousin, Nicholas Blasingame. *Doctor* Nicholas Blasingame. He has consented to visit for a few months and try his hand at being a country doctor. I hope nothing makes him decide to leave us."

There was something in her tone that made the warning tingle move again inside Nick. Something was being conveyed, very diplomatically, to the sheriff.

Nicholas took the man's offered hand and shook it. "Happy to meet you, Sheriff. I suspect we'll be working together a bit, from what Alicia writes about the accident rate, not to mention the fights."

Tolliver spat into the gutter, the stream of brown tobacco juice disappearing into the darkness. "Could be. Maybe not. If I see anybody needs a doctor, I'll tell 'em you're here." The tone was grudging, and the man's scar-tracked face was wary and vaguely hostile.

Bart took Alicia's arm. "We've got to get our cousin home and feed him before he falls flat. Be seeing you, Sheriff." The prospect seemed to lack enticement; he sounded unenthusiastic.

They made their way through the incredibly muddy area teeming with wagons and buggies to reach a modest rig that was sheltered by a black bonnet-like hood that kept off the rain. Bart bundled the baggage into the rear, as Nick helped Alicia climb into the high seat. As she mounted, her reticule swung against his lifted arm.

Again Nick was startled. There was something heavy. Compact. Deadly. In that familiar black velvet pouch was a pistol. Alicia, too, was carrying a revolver. He looked up to meet her gaze. She gathered her skirts and motioned to him to climb up beside her.

When Bart had mounted the other side and carefully guided the two sorrels out of the crowded freight yard, Nick looked across his cousin at the younger man. Bart was staring down the muddy rut track, seeming to see nothing but the swinging circle of light from the lantern and the horses' rumps and the black forest rising beyond the lantern's range. The warm mood of welcome seemed to have leached away in that brief encounter with the sheriff. Nick was determined to find the reason.

"All right, my dears," he said, "I haven't lived for thirty-five years without leaning anything at all. What in the world is the matter back there in town? And why are you both at odds with the sheriff?"

Alicia sighed and took his hand between both of hers. "I had hoped you'd be able to settle in, get a good look at the country and the people, before you had to run into this...this thing. We didn't know what was the matter for a couple of months or more, isn't that right, Bart?"

"Not for sure. But we did suspect something was amiss. You know we did," her husband answered. He was turning the horses toward a barely discernible lighter gap in the darkness along the edge of the road.

16

They squished through heavy mud into a lane leading directly into a stable yard. Bart cramped the buggy close to a stone block, where his passengers dismounted and found a path of packed earth that was only faintly muddy.

"Jimmy will get the horses. Come on, Nick, you take the lantern and your medical bag. I'll bring the rest of your traps. Al will show you the way, and I'll be right behind. We'll tell you the long, sad tale after supper. It isn't a thing you want to hear about on an empty stomach."

Nick followed his cousin along a mass of dripping greenery onto a porch. There was glass in the door, through which a faint gleam shone. A light behind it grew brighter, as a lamp was brought at Alice's call.

"Carry-Ann, this is Mr. Nick, my cousin. He needs something hot and filling as soon as we can get it on the table. I'm going to my room to change my shoes, but I'll be there to help you soon." She turned Nick over to a small plump Negress, who led him to a room at the left of the huge entry foyer, while the Hazel tons moved away to the right.

"Ain't no weather for staying damp, Mr. Nick," she said, opening a white painted door and setting one of his bags inside. "They's fresh water and towels. You wash up and change to something dry. Supper's ready; just needs dishing up and putting on the table."

Nick touched her elbow as she turned to leave. "Carry-Ann, how's Alicia doing? I mean really? She looks well, but something seems to be worrying her. That's not good in her situation."

The little woman looked up at him, her head

cocked hack, her brown eyes sizing him up with what he was sure was unerring accuracy. She nodded, as if satisfied. "Thought you might be one of them high-and-mighty Yankee folks," she said. "But I sees you isn't. She's fine. Eats good. Sleeps pretty good, when that man ain't giving Mr. Bart no trouble. She'd be in first-class shape, if it wasn't for them po' white trash in town." She turned to leave. "You got about ten minutes to get ready for supper. I goes home to my family at night."

Nick took the hint. He found himself standing in the narrow dining room in quite a bit less than the allotted time. Now that he had an opportunity to look about him, he realized that the house was quite presentable, for one built in so new a country. A wide hallway down the middle had been closed from the weather by the glassed door in front, flanked by etched-glass panels. At the back it was also closed by French doors.

On the side where his room was there were also the dining room and the capacious kitchen. He felt certain that on the other were the main bedroom, Bart's office, and a spare room. The dining room was not really as narrow as its high ceiling made it appear. He recalled Alicia writing him that in this muggy climate high ceilings were a necessity, if one were to survive the summer heat.

A sound in the hall made him turn to greet a small skinny man who looked to be either mulatto or part Indian. "You must be Jimmy," Nick said.

The little man looked him over with the self-assurance that he had noted among most of the people, high and low, whom he had met in traveling through this part of the country. Finishing his survey, Jimmy said, "You Doctor Nick. We wait a long time to see you. Good you come. We need doctor, sometimes mighty bad. Just don't let…." His words trailed off as Alicia and Bart opened their door and came into the hall.

Jimmy turned to Bart and assured him that the horses had been cared for. He nodded again to Nick and left, leaving the physician to wonder what he had been about to say.

Alicia, however, took his arm and turned with him into the dining room. "Sit here with Bart, while I get some food onto this table!" she commanded.

He grinned across the table. "Is she always this bossy?" he asked. Bart's square face wrinkled into an answering smile. "If I didn't have her to do the book work for the store I'd be lost," he said. "Besides, I never did have gumption. I needed a smart girl who could keep my nose to the grindstone. And my tail out of cracks," he added thoughtfully.

"What is the trouble, Bart?" Nick asked, leaning forward into the lamplight that flooded the white linen cloth with mellow gold. "I can see that the place has been good for my cousin. For you, too. You both look so much stronger than you did. Not to mention that you have gained an assurance that, to be honest, I never would have thought you'd develop back in the days when you dogged my coattails like a faithful pup. What does the sheriff have against you? He even looked daggers at Alicia, and God knows she could never hurt a fly."

"Don't be too sure of that," Bart said. "Since we've been here, Al's learned a lot of things they don't teach at Miss Chesterton's School for Young Ladies of Good Family. Three nights ago she was working late on the books while I unpacked new stock. Somebody evidently I thought she was in the store alone. He wireworked the lock on the front door and tried to grab her. She shot him twice...once in each leg."

Nick looked at the young man, his expression incredulous. "*Alicia?* Deliberately? In both legs? She can't shoot!"

"She can now," Bart said. He rose to help his wife set the big tureen of stew in the middle of the table. "She can hit the center of a tin can lid at a hundred paces with a Colt. With either hand. So can I. It's...necessary, with things as they are."

"But there is law here. Why not turn it over to the sheriff I just met? He may not be friendly, but that is his job. Not yours, surely."

Alicia surveyed her table, nodded to Carry-Ann, and said, "You can go home, dear. I do appreciate your staying to help me. Tell David I thank him, too." She waited until the little woman had left. Then she turned to Nick.

"Tolliver's deputy is the man I shot. We have been robbed three times. Sometimes they take ammunition, sometimes hardware. Whatever any of them happen to need. Nobody in town ever calls the law when they are robbed, because they know good and well that it was the law that robbed them. Tell him, Bart."

Her husband dipped his spoon into the stew and stirred it thoughtfully. "The first time was just after I opened the store. I had stocked a silver-mounted saddle. I intended to have a drawing to build business, in a few weeks. It came in, and I stuck it up on a stand beside the front door so everyone could take

20

a look at it. Two nights later, the door was broken in and the saddle was stolen. Nothing else was taken, just that.

"The minute I found what had happened, I lit out for the sheriff's office. His horse was hitched in front, and the saddle was cinched on it. I looked at that saddle right there in broad daylight in front of the sheriff's office, bold as brass, and I understood a lot of things. We're not fools. If that was the way it was, then we had to learn to cope with it."

"But we didn't have to like it," said Alicia, ladling more stew into Nick's bowl. "We've made it clear we don't, and we don't make it easy for the crooks to rob us. And that, my dear cousin, is why Sheriff Tolliver was less than joyful at having another of our family come to Moreno."

The rain had begun again, tapping light fingers against the glass behind Nick. He looked about the lamp-lit room, at its quiet elegance so like Alicia. He looked at her fair face, composed and ladylike as ever, and thought that she had shot a man...and she showed no sign of being sorry about that.

It was a strange new world into which he had come.

CHAPTER TWO

As he lay in the unfamiliar bed, listening to a babble of varied screaks, hums, chitters, and calls that challenged the musical scale in virtuosity, Nick found himself unable to sleep immediately. The long limbo of his trip from Baltimore had ended in something so strange it left him feeling disoriented.

The expression on Alicia's face as they talked of her encounter with the amorous deputy, as well as the obvious pride that Bart felt at her ability to take care of herself—those things challenged the civilized upbringing that all three of them had shared. That troubled him.

Yet at last he drifted off. The bed was a good one, and the tap of the rain on the roof and the windows soothed his weary nerves. When he woke, sunlight was pouring through his windows, lighting the simple room. He lay for a while, looking about at the familiar furniture that Alicia had brought from their grandmother's house. The gargoyle above the dressing table grinned at the one topping the tall head of the bed. The marble shone with polishing, and he suspected that Carry-Ann's hands had done that chore.

There came the sound of whistling from outside,

the stables. He shook himself fully awake and ready to greet this first day of what he hoped be a new life. A clatter in the direction of the kitchen made him hurry, for his stomach was growling, unhappy with the greasy and ill-cooked meals he imposed upon it as he traveled.

When he stuck his face in the kitchen door, the Negress smiled up at him from behind a marble-topped table on which she was working biscuit dough.

"Look like you slept mighty good," she observed, pummeling the floury mass. She stroked it flat on the table. "First night, most folks hears the frogs and the crickets goin' on so loud they can't doze off. You must of been mighty tired."

He sighed. "That stew of yours last night made my stomach so happy that I went off to sleep like a full baby. Now I'm hungry again. Could I help you with something?" He looked around the spick-and-span kitchen.

"You really wants to, you kin set the table. Mornings, we serves in here. The folks got to get off to work early, and it saves time. Here—you can find plates up in this here cabinet. Glasses is behind you in the glass cabinet."

Nick bustled around, putting plates and utensils on the round table that filled the space between the two windows that lit the kitchen from the east. Something about Carry-Ann filled the place that had been left empty by the death years ago of his old black nurse Zilda. She had the same no-nonsense way, the same warmth. He was more than glad to find Alicia in her capable hands.

As he busied himself, he found himself thinking

again about that conversation of the night before. Finished, he sat on a tall stool beside the marble-topped work table.

"Carry-Ann," he said, "I don't want to gossip—don't think that—but I can't help being worried over what they told me last night—about Alicia's shooting that deputy. Are things really so bad here? Is the sheriff truly an outlaw, or have my cousins just gotten off on the wrong foot with him?"

Carry-Ann used the biscuit cutter with painstaking precision, avoiding his eyes. "It's bad; she admitted. "Worse for the black folks than it is for the whites. Been going on for a long time too. Tolliver's cousin, Caz Whitfield, takes turns with him being sheriff. Every time folks gets fed up with one of 'em, the other steps in and gets to be sheriff. Makes no mind how folks votes, either. One or t'other of 'em gets it." She pounded another batch of dough flat with a dark fist.

"They steals from everybody. They rapes folks, if they thinks they can get away with it. If Miss Al hadn't of shot that man, he'd of raped her for sure. Nobody could or would of done nothing about it. She'd never of got over it. You know her, I 'spect. How she is. And her being pregnant—it'd just have purely killed her."

Nick stole a snippet of dough, and Carry slapped his hand lightly just as Zilda used to do.

"I know her pretty well," he answered, savoring the dough. "But I thought for sure she could never have shot anybody, or even brought herself to fire a gun. I can see that she had to do it, if things are the way you say, but she's changed. Changed a lot."

"Let me tell you something, Mr. Nick. Make

you see how it is, here. I got a auntie. She mighty ol', now. Was born a slave and growed up one. Her white folks was mighty good to her; taken care of her always. When ol' Mr. Greening died a few years ago, he put some money in a bank to take care of her for the rest of her life. And he left her a little bit of spending money right out.

"She lived close to town, and she was still spry enough to walk to it. So she did, and they give her fifty dollars in fives and ones. She stopped at the store and put a couple of dollars in her shoe. Then she taken out for home.

"Hadn't got more than halfway when one of them deputies come running after her on his horse—taken all the money out of her purse. She hated that, but she wasn't a bit surprised, so she kept right on walking. Befo' she could get home, that deputy come running back. The teller at the bank had told him there was more, and they wasn't about to miss it. He shaken her down till he found the two dollars in her shoe. Then he was satisfied." She checked the pan of biscuits in the oven of the wood-burning stove.

"That's just once that I'm telling you about. Hit happens all the time. Mostly to black folks, cause it takes a heap of robbin' to get anything much outen us. They gets big stuff off the white folks what owns stores and farms and cattle."

Nick stood as she thrust another pan of biscuits into the waiting oven. He opened he door behind him to admit Alicia.

She came in briskly, apologizing to Carry-Ann. "I'm so sorry, Carry. I just had a time getting to sleep, and then it seemed I couldn't wake up. Then

Bart slipped out early and didn't wake me, either. What do we lack doing?"

"We's just about got it done, Miz Al. You set yourself dawn on that stool and visit with your cousin, while I watches the biscuits. He done set the table already. The ham's in the oven, and the scrambled eggs won't take no time at all when Mr. Bart comes in."

Sitting on the stool, Alicia looked a radiant twenty, though she was, in fact, twenty-eight. She not only bloomed with her pregnancy, she radiated good health and sturdy self-reliance. It seemed that she had become an entirely different woman from the fragile wisp who had defied her family's wrath to follow Bart here.

"I'm glad you did," Nick said, following his thoughts into words.

As usual, Alicia caught his meaning at once. "So'm I," she said. "I'd have spent my life in Baltimore alternating between bouts of illness and periods of frantic frustration. I just wasn't cut out to be a proper Baltimore lady, Nick. You remember the things I used to do at school!"

He burst into laughter. "Miss Atherton came to Gramma once. She'd talked with your parents and found they couldn't control your terrible sense of humor. I was in medical school at the time, and I stayed with Gramma quite often to save traveling so far back and forth to' the farm. I was studying in the library, and they had their conference in Gramma's little reading roam. Once I knew what they were talking about, I eavesdropped shamelessly. Even went and stood looking through a slit in the draperies that covered the doorway."

He chuckled. "She was so upset. You'd gone through the teachers' quarters and poured molasses between their sheets. Nobody escaped your attention except the little woman who taught dancing—what was her name?—and Madame du Valière.

"Gramma was trying to keep her face properly straight and sympathetic and concerned, but I could see her laugh wrinkles getting deeper and deeper at the corners of her eyes. I've often wondered why you spared those two teachers?"

"Easy," said Alicia, hopping down from the stool to meet Bart, who came in smelling of the green outdoors. "Miss Drinker was fun. And Madame was pitiful. The rest were idiots. Full of useless rules about proper decorum and insane homilies about letting a chair in which a young man had sat cool off before sitting in it yourself. I wonder now if any of them had the remotest idea where babies come from." She grinned at Bart, who winked in return. The three sat down amid laughter.

The meal was ample and delicious, but they didn't dawdle over it. The Hazeltons were due at the store. Nick intended to spend the day there with them, meeting any townsfolk who happened in. He found himself with a touch of the "first day of school" excitement he had thought himself too mature ever to feel again.

By day, the short distance between the Hazeltons' home and Moreno was a delight. The sun struck at angles through the masses of branches, now clad in spring green. Now and again a circle of white interrupted the vibrant foliage, and Alicia would gaze until she could see it no longer.

"Dogwood," she breathed. "If that were not such

an unromantic name. and if the child should be a girl, I'd like to name it after that tree. It should have been called something beautiful—out of Shakespeare, perhaps."

* * * * * * *

The ride seemed too short, this time. They found themselves soon in the back street that led to the livery stable, where the wagon was lined up against a wall with several others. The horses were turned over to a sleepy boy to be put into stalls and fed.

When they arrived, the street was empty, but by the time they reached the door of the mercantile, a few horsemen had appeared. A wagon or two now trundled into sight, and doors of several businesses began to open. There seemed very few of these, in contrast with the vast wilderness through which Nick had traveled. Yet with that expanse in mind, Moreno seemed almost over-large.

He could see, from his position before the mercantile's doorway, a bakery, a milliner dressmaker's shop, and a grocery store. Across the way, the sheriff's office was hard by the saloon, an arrangement that would have made a lot of sense, given lawmen who did their job properly. An empty storefront was directly across from the mercantile, and beside it was the office of a dentist-barber.

Alicia appeared at his shoulder. Her gaze followed his. "Old Doc Pinter has been the only medical man here for a long time. He hates anything except cutting hair and pulling teeth, and he'll be overjoyed to find you here. He came in here one morning all torn up. He been called out in the middle of the night to deliver a baby, and both the child and its mother died. He swore he'd never let anybody talk him into such a thing again. He knew only what he'd gathered from his other cases, and the problems were just too much for him. I'll take you across the street, when he comes in, and introduce you. He has room in his place for an office, if you'd like be right there where people are used to going."

It sounded sensible. When a portly little man appeared to unlock the door, he called to Alicia, "Can you spare the time? He's there."

"Better now than later, when things will be busy," she said. "Come on."

Dr. Pinter had one of those cherubic faces whose contours conceal the sharp shrewdness of their eyes. Its hue hinted more at drink than good health, but there was no sign of degeneration in the man's speech or thinking.

He looked up at Nick, as Alicia made her way between two wagons to return to the store. "You will never know, sir, how much I appreciate the fact that you have come. When Mrs. Hazelton told me you were coming, I was glad for her. When I heard her say you were a doctor, I was glad for myself. I have been beset, sir, veritably beset by injured miners, farmers who have been kicked halfway to kingdom come by their own livestock, and women with breech deliveries. God deliver me from ever attending another! Come inside, sir, let us talk."

Nick found that the little man, by dint of involuntary experience and his own native intelligence, was a fair diagnostician. Nick suspected that he had done more than fairly by those who had come into his hands. They sat for an hour, and in that time

Nick found himself with a good picture of the state of the town's health.

This farmer was going to have a stroke in time, and there was nothing Pinter could think of to make him slow down. That woman would never conceive, though she was always on the alert for any quack remedy that might change her condition.

"But the nastiest things you'll come up against," Pinter told him, rising to meet a black man who came groaning into the office, holding his jaw, "is the mine injury. That outfit can find more ways to break bones and crush bodies than anything I ever heard of. The Morans, bad cess to them, squeeze the last grain of profit from the working people, but they never try to make the workings safer." His face was even pinker than usual with the force of his emotion.

"Those killed or disabled for life are dismissed as necessary operating losses. Not one widow or orphan has ever, to my knowledge, received a thin dime from the company as indemnity."

He settled the man into his dentist's chair, looked into his mouth, said, "Oho!" and reached in with his forceps. There came a sharp jerk. The man yelled, and Pinter brandished a bloody tooth.

"There she is, Amos. You'll feel good as new in just a bit. Here." He filled a shot glass from a brown bottle and the smell of good whiskey filled the air.

Amos, smiling broadly, downed the drink, placed a wad of gauze in his jaw, and looked down at the little dentist.

"Two chickens enough, Doctor?" he asked.

"That'll be fine, Amos. I certainly would like a bit of Mandy's sausage, come fall and hog-killing time. You suppose you could throw in a pound or two of that?"

"Sho' kin, Doc. You jest remind me when de time comes." Amos settled his teeth against the wad and left Dr. Pinter and Nick alone in the office.

"You will find, young doctor Nick, that you will be paid in produce far more than in money here. There is in fact, very little cash, and what there is, usually sticks in the pockets of the Morans, the Tollivers, and the Whitfields. With a great imbalance in favor of the Morans, of course. They use the alternating sheriffs for their own purposes, which are seldom if ever simon-pure. In return, they assure their continuance in office, whatever the will of the local electorate. The governor owes them political debts, so any protest aimed state-ward is sent, straightaway, back to the sheriff, who proceeds to pistol-whip the protester."

Nick stared at him, surprised that he was willing to confide such things to someone who might lighten his load. Pinter chuckled. "You're from the cynical North, my boy. I'd like myself little, if I let you settle yourself into this den of iniquity without giving you some warning. Besides which, you impress me as being a man who does what he thinks is right, not what seems most immediately profitable. And your cousins, brave and bright as they are, will need your help. They are making money from their store. That will soon come to the notice of the powers that be. Then the Hazeltons will have problems maybe more than they can handle."

"I appreciate your candor, Dr. Pinter," Nick said, rising and moving toward the door. "I ran into municipal dishonesty back in Baltimore. I was too innocent and ignorant to fight it intelligently, then. I'm older, now, and trickier—who is that?" he interrupted himself to ask, as the man he had seen on the train came into sight on the sidewalk.

Pinter moved up beside him and adjusted his glasses. "I met the man last night at the saloon. His name, if I recallcorrectly, is William Exeter St. John. Britisher, without any doubt. Eyes like chilled shot. He seemed thick With Tolliver. Didn't say what his business might be in this area."

Nick frowned. "I saw him on the train. He struck me oddly. I think he's a bad one, without any evidence for the opinion at all. I hate to think I'm superstitious but he made a rabbit bit run over my grave when I happened to catch his eye."

"Anybody Tolliver is cultivating is a good person to stay away from," grunted the little dentist. "Though he strikes me more as one of the Morans would find admirable. He's a cut or two above the Tollivers and Whitfields."

A woman came into the office, shepherding four little boys. The men moved aside, and she settled the children on the long bench in front of the combination barbershop and dentist's chair.

"They've all got to have haircuts, Doc. And I've got shopping to do. Can you deal with them while I get it done?" she asked.

Pinter nodded. "Glad to, Millie. Just wish all the young 'uns here were as well behaved as yours. That's why I give you a discount. I've never been bit by a one of your boys. You go on and tend to your business. We'll be done in less than an hour."

He looked up at Nick and smiled. "I like the children. Even the ones that bite. It's a lot of the adults that I find exasperating. Why don't these people hang them a sheriff?"

As recently as yesterday Nick would have found the idea shocking. Now he found himself wondering the same thing as he wandered up the street, nodding to strangers who would soon, he hoped, be patients.

If Alicia and Bart were left to resist the set-up alone, he could foresee bad things in the future. In that short time he made up his mind. Whatever the situation, he had run for the last time. Moreno would be his home, come what might.

CHAPTER THREE

As the streets filled, Nick found his way back to the mercantile, and stood beside the window where Alicia's cash box shared desk space with her ledgers. She would look up, now and then when a shadow darkened the glass, and give Nick the name, family history, probable destination, and moral character of the passerby, before he was out of sight. This amused her cousin mightily.

"I thought Baltimore was the world capital of gossip, but this beats the old city by a mile," he chuckled. "How in the world do you find out and keep up with all this stuff?"

She counted out change into the grubby palm of a small boy and helped him to settle his lumpy burden of screws, nails, and bolts. Instead of answering directly, she nodded toward the child's departing back.

"That's Isaiah Crow. His father is our cabinetmaker. His shop is on the short street where the livery stable is. His mother was Maddalena Elisia Carmela Moreno. Her great-grandfather was the first Spanish alcalde, here. Her family is pure Spanish and was very prominent back in Spain. So her child, being half Spanish, is referred to as 'that

Mex'kin kid of old Isaiah Crow's' and looked down upon because of his noble heritage."

She sighed. "His father is a fine craftsman. His mother was a lovely lady by all accounts. But he is and always will be considered a Mexican by our 'enlightened' fellow whites. Which doesn't, of course, answer your question." She paused to go back to the dress and fabric counter to help a fat young woman decide on a bolt of calico.

She returned with the bolt of cloth and an expression of distaste. "Can you visualize six little red-headed girls dressed identically in purple calico with orange flowers? That woman! I have some lovely dark blue with lavender, but she wouldn't consider it. She, by the way, is one the town's leading lights. Her father is the butcher, her husband one of Tolliver's deputies...and her brother the amorous soul I shot a while back. If you tell her anything— anything whatsoever—she will make a highly insulting story of it.

"She will then go and tell her inaccurate version to everyone concerned, thereby making you an enemy for life. Don't so much as mention that Mrs. Jones has a lovely house—not to her. Mrs. Jones will be at your throat by the time Emily Thrasher gets done with ornamenting your comment.

"And that, I suppose, is one of the reasons we all keep a close check on one another. You have to learn the people to avoid, the ones with whom you can talk freely as well, in a town of this size. We live cheek by jowl almost literally." She laughed softly.

"You may be amused to learn that Bart and I are being ostracized, right now, by the Thrashers' set.

35

Not because I shot her brother, though that is part of it. But mostly because we went to supper at the Crows'. We like both father and son, and we don't like the social bigwigs here. Of course, once I shot her kin, she all but holds her nose when she gets near me. Only the fact that we have the only dry goods and hardware store in town brings her in here."

Nick observed the plump woman as she browsed through the yard goods and went on to the ribbons. He shuddered when she picked up a bolt of scarlet satin ribbon and headed for the desk. Six little redheads in purple, orange, and scarlet!

Anyway, now he knew how to approach the woman. A doctor had to get along with everyone to some extent, and he had no intention of running afoul of her.

"And this must be your cousin," she was saying, as she laid the ribbon beside the calico. "A doctor, they say. Her tone was dubious.

"Yes, I am," Nick said, smiling.

"How nice. Moreno has needed someone a bit more presentable than poor old Doctor Pinter for a long time. I hope you will honor us with a visit, now that we have been introduced." She smiled, but her hard blue eyes were assessing the cost of his broadcloth coat, the cut of his silk tie, and the quality of his linen. He expected her to peer under the desk in order to examine his boots, but she didn't...quite.

"It will be some time before I am able to be sociable," he said, handing her the brown-wrapped package. "I do appreciate the invitation."

When the wide back had waddled from view, Alicia collapsed into her chair, shaking with laughter. "I would never have believed that Nicholas Blasingame, fiery Nick, could stand there with a smile on his face and be politely noncommittal to that...woman!" she gasped, wiping her eyes on the sunshine-yellow pinafore that she wore in the store.

"I learned a lot that last year in Baltimore," he said, his tone dry. Then he peered out at the street. "What's going on out there?" he asked.

Alicia craned her neck to see. "Oh, Lord!" she said. All trace of laughter was gone. "It's that infernal Brockner boy. He starts drinking as soon as the saloon opens, and by noon he's usually well and truly tipsy. Bart!"

Her husband appeared from the stockroom. "Hobie Brockner is about to make trouble for David," she said to him. "I can tell by the way he's acting. We can't let anything happen to David. He's our friend and Carry Ann's husband. But we're in such bad odor with the law now, I don't know what we should do. Can you think of anything remotely tactful?"

A spatter of shots interrupted her. Nick could now see a tall, slender black man walking with dignity down the edge of the dusty street, avoiding the puddles remaining from the rain earlier. His back was bowed under the weight of a gunnysack, but his head was held proudly. He was paying no heed to the heckling of a husky blond boy who kept pace, step for step, on the boardwalk at elbow.

As Nick watched, the young man fired off three shots, aimed to miss, just barely, David's boot heels.

Nick moved, with his curious neatness of motion, to the door and onto the walkway. As the youngster paused to reload his revolver, the physi-

37

cian reached a long arm and took the gun from him.

"Drunks and children shouldn't play with loaded guns," he observed quietly. His dark-blue eyes held a spark that belied his tone. "That puts you two down. You can pick this up at the mercantile when you sober up."

He turned on his heel to reenter the store as the boy swung. The blow glanced off his shoulder, upsetting his balance. Even while regaining it, he was swinging around on his steady foot, the other one extended to take the boy's legs out from under him.

The young man went down into a fuddled heap. Nick caught him by the coat collar and pulled him up. Then he frog-marched him toward the sheriff's office. "I am preferring charges against this man," he told the startled deputy behind the desk. "Public drunkenness. Creating a disturbance. Discharge of firearm inside a township. Assault on an innocent bystander. Lock him up, will you?"

Sheriff Tolliver hurried into the office from a back room. "No need for all that hooraw. Hobie's just been havin' a little fun, that's all. No harm in stirrin' up a nigger a little bit. He ain't hurt none. Nobody around here pays no never mind to old Hobie. Just a fun-lovin' boy, he is."

"You refuse to charge him as I requested?" Nick asked. He knew the answer already.

"Well, not rightly refuse," the sheriff said. "More like—I'm trying to explain to you how things're done around here. We don't lock up white boys for upsettin' niggers. Course, he really shouldn't of shot off his piece right here in town. That kin be dangerous, and I appreciate you stoppin' him. But otherwise, let's just forget everything. All right?"

Nick looked straight into the man's eyes. "All right," he said. They both knew that a challenge had given and accepted.

Nick left Hobie to the sheriff's tender mercies and hurried across the street to the mercantile. David had found refuge inside, and Nick found him in earnest conversation with Bart.

"Nick, this is David. He wants me to tell you that he's truly appreciative of what you did, but he wishes you hadn't taken the chance." David's dark, thin face was red with worry lines as he nodded.

"If you gets yourself in bad wid de sheriff," he said, "and he and de rest won't lie easy till they gets you back, it'll be bad. And we needs a doctor, sir."

"Don't worry, David. I've butted heads with much tougher men than your sheriff. Ask Alicia. She'll tell that I'm the world's worst hardhead. If I'm going to be working here in Moreno, those people over there at the sheriff's office have got to learn that I do what I think right. No matter what they think about it!"

After David had gone on his way to the grist mill with last of his old crop of corn for grinding, Alicia turned to her cousin. "I thought you had learned to avoid confrontations, Nick. After the time you have had in Baltimore, I would have thought you'd never take another chance of getting in wrong with officials."

"Why Allie, I haven't shot a one of them yet," he teased. "So far, you're two legs up on me, though I doubt I'll ever come to shooting with that crew. I've learned a lot, you're right there, but putting up with nastiness in order to stay in good with officialdom isn't part of that. I'm smarter now than I used to be. A lot sneakier, too." He grinned at her, and she smiled back reluctantly. Her eyes, however, were still shadowed with worry.

"Don't fret, little Coz. You'll have your baby wearing wrinkle lines before he's born. You need to stay calm and happy for the next few months."

"Easy to say!" she returned. "It's just that there are so many injustices and stupidities around here. Bart and I just can't seem to stay out of them, when we think we might be able to help."

He grunted. "Have you had any trouble, aside from your run-in with the burglar, with the law? Anything serious since they stole that saddle? Does anything give you the feeling they might be planning to hit you hard?"

Bart, trundling past with a rack of harness, said, "No. That surprises me a bit, too." He set the rack against the front wall and straightened the hanging leather and metal. "Everyone else has had a lot of problems since we came. If they've taken anything more from us, it's something so small we didn't miss it."

"Once you understood the problem—after the saddle incident—did you ever have any words with Tolliver? Telling him how you stood, so to speak?"

Bart blushed. "As a matter of fact, I did. He had been in the bakery and came out with an armload of cakes and pastries. Mrs. Flanders was raising Cain, inside, and her husband was just standing there like a whipped dog. I went up to Tolliver and said, 'Don't think it would be this way if you came into my store' or something of the kind. 'My wife and I don't put up with such things, and don't you forget

40

it!' I meant it, too. Had blood in my eye, for Mrs. Flanders is such a hard-working little soul, and her husband didn't even try to take up for her."

He chuckled harshly. "Tolliver saw right then and there that he wasn't going to be able to go about his usual run of business quietly and without any fuss, so he hasn't bothered us again."

"Makes sense," mused Nick. "If everyone else did the same thing and meant it, even to the extent of being willing to bleed a bit to prove it, this kind of town couldn't exist." He patted Alicia's shoulder. "Maybe you haven't too much to worry about. I hope I scared him off for good. But for God's sake, don't drop your guard!" What he didn't say was the thing that worried him most. What if Tolliver had reached a similar conclusion and realized that one successful set of rebels against his tyranny might give others mutinous notions? That gave rise to worrisome thoughts, but Nick concealed them as they prepared to close the store for the night.

It was still fully light, for the spring days had lengthened. The sun was not yet down to the tops of the trees in the west. The light slanted into the big windows, and Nick, at Alicia's direction, lowered a grid of ironwork behind the big panes, locking it into place with latches all the way around.

"We don't intend to lose anything else," Bart said with some satisfaction. "If you think that's stout, you should see the way I have the back entry fixed up."

As they locked the front door, Doc Pinter waved from across the street. "Doctor Blasingame! Doctor Blasingame! I've a patient for you! Her husband just rode up. Hermann! Here's the doctor. You take him right on out. Lucy's going to be fine, now!" He sighed and wiped his flushed forehead.

"You just don't know how wonderful it is to have a real physician here. I'm so relieved not to be responsible for things I'm not qualified to do."

Nick nodded to the big German who waited beside Pinter. "My bag's in the wagon at the livery, sir. Won't take a minute to get it, but I'll have to rent a horse. Doctor Pinter, don't you think it might comfort the gentleman's wife if you came, too? Just for the ride, and to make her feel better, having someone she knows along with a stranger."

Pinter frowned. Then he nodded. "I suppose you're right, Doctor. She is a bit nervous and notional. It would probably calm her nerves to have me there while you do the work. I'll go to the livery with you, and we can ride together in my buggy. You really must get one, by the way. Most necessary. You can sleep while your horse goes on your rounds automatically, once you have him trained. Without such a chance to rest, you'd seldom get much sleep, I guarantee that."

So it was that Nick climbed into Pinter's excellent buggy and waved goodbye to his cousins. Once again he was feeling that anticipatory sense he had felt that morning. His first patient waited for him!

"This is Hermann Wald," Pinter told him, as they started up the narrow street, with Wald riding beside their wheel. "He's foreman out at the mine. His wife cooks for the Morans, when she's able. She worked until just a little while ago, isn't that right, Hermann?"

"Ja. She stoud voomans, mine Lucy. But now she have troobles. Baby not come yet. It be two days. She get veak. The black voomans at the mine know not vot to do, now."

Nick shuddered. Beside him, he felt Pinter shiver too. Two days of labor! What would they find when they arrived? Surely there was great need for a doctor hereabout, he mused, as the black mare tripped daintily along the hard-packed road, from which all trace of rain or mud had been beaten by the constant passage of traffic.

Wald's home was one of four identical frame shanties lined up beside the fence surrounding the entire mine area. Down the road a short distance a clutter of even less presentable houses sheltered many small black children at the moment.

From the interior of the house before which they stopped could be heard a quiet moaning. The black woman who met them on the porch wore an expression of deep gloom.

"She ain't come yet," she said to Wald. "She all dry, and de child's all messed up inside her. Cain't get ahold of it. She gwine die, Mr. Wald."

Nicholas pushed past the pair, followed by Pinter. Now that the time had come, the little man seemed eager to do what he could to help. There was only one bedroom, and Lucy Wald lay on a sweat-and blood-soaked mattress on an iron bedstead that took up most of the room in the tiny chamber.

Pinter bent over the woman and took her hand. "Lucy, girl, it's old Doc. I've come to help you, and I've brought a real doctor with me. This is Doctor Blasingame. He can do things I don't even know the names of."

Her eyes, iris-blue, opened for an instant. Her

fair face was mottled and sweaty, but she tried to smile. *"Danke,"* she croaked. Then her eyes closed, and her body convulsed.

Nick lifted her in his arms. "Pull those dirty sheets off, Doc. See if there are any clean ones."

The black woman came with an armful of ragged but clean linen. She made up the bed, while Nick held the tortured body in his arms. Then he laid his burden gently back on the bed and turned to Doc. "I've got to do a caesarean," he said. "It's pretty much of a last resort in this case, but she's not going to last much longer like this. Can you give the ether?"

Pinter paled, but he nodded. He went out to convey to the woman their need for hot water and strong soap. In short order, the pair found themselves scrubbing up. Meanwhile, the woman arranged oilcloth beneath the patient...and Nick was pleased to see it was a new piece, clean. That was good.

It was a terribly long evening. Lucy was so exhausted that the ether took effect quickly. The operation was relatively simple, but trying to piece her back together was another thing entirely. The struggles of the child to be born and of Lucy's body to expel it had torn and twisted and mauled her internally.

At last, Nick called for Hermann, who was waiting on the porch for the outcome. "I can remove her womb," he told the man, "and she will stand some chance of living. If I try to mend it and leave it inside, she'll die of infection. It's pretty certain. Either way, you'll have no more children. You name it."

Hermann's round blue eyes welled full of tears.

He looked past Nick at his pale wife on the bed. "Do vat's best, Doctor. Mine Lucy is goot vooman. Dere are many *kinder* ve can raise, but only vun Lucy."

Nick sighed with relief. When he was finished stitching his patient up, he heard with much surprise the fragile cry of an infant.

"You don't mean it's alive!" he whispered to Pinter, who had just reentered the room.

"Just a little trick I invented," the small man said with pride. "I don't know the rules, so I have just done what looked sensible, as the need arose. So when I delivered a baby that couldn't breathe— or didn't seem to want to—I just squeezed it gently to pump air into it.

"Sometimes it worked, sometimes it didn't. This time it did." His expression was so triumphant that Nick broke into a chuckle. He hurried into the main room of the little house to meet his new patient.

Hermann was standing in the middle of the tiny room, as the black woman held the infant for him to see. "Is a boy," he said to Nick. "He's alive, the liddle fellow. I think he die, for sure."

"So did I," answered Nick. "You can thank Doc Pinter here that he didn't. But about your wife—I just can't say for sure. Who is the best woman to nurse around here?"

Pinter grunted. "I'm no woman, but I'm an excellent nurse. I'll stay here until Lucy is better—or not. Don't worry, Doctor Nick. You go home in my buggy, and you can pick me up tomorrow when you come to check on her."

Nick drove homeward in pitch darkness. Stars blazed above the needled crests of the pines. Weary

as he was, worried about many things, he knew he
had never felt better in his life.

CHAPTER FOUR

When Nick awoke, he knew it was late. The morning sun had already moved past his window, and the feel of lateness was in him. He stretched and rose. From the hallway, which served as living room-parlor of the house, he could hear a soft clinking, together with an almost inaudible humming. Carry-Ann; he felt certain, was dusting as quietly as she could manage, in order not to wake him.

"I'm awake," he called. "Did Allie tell you that the Walds have a boy? And Mrs. Wald, I hope and pray, may live?"

He opened his door to see Carry's back disappearing into the kitchen. "You come on in here and tell me about it whilst I fixes your breakfast," she demanded, slicing a loaf of bread and spreading butter lavishly onto the slices.

She slid the pan into the oven to toast. "I thought you'd be waking up about now, so I went ahead and fired up the stove," she said, breaking three eggs into a blue bowl and whipping them to foam, along with a dollop of thick cream. "You tell me, now, about how Miz Lucy's doing."

Nick hunkered down to keep an eye on his toast. "I hope to God she's better this morning. Doc Pinter, bless his soul, volunteered to stay out there and take care of her all night. He's as good a doctor as many I've met who had the training, from what I can see. So if there's any chance at all for her, she's got the right care. I'm going out in a while to check on her and bring him back to town. Do you know anybody who would take a turn at staying with her? She will need a lot of nursing, yet, if she makes it."

Carry chuckled. "Miz Allie, she say I'm to go and stay wid her for a while. I done birthed more babies and took care of more sick folks than a dog has fleas. She say wid just the three of you, she can make out fine till I gets back. Most folks hereabouts have got too many chillun to take care of, or they got a mean man that don't want to do for hisself for a day or two. But David and me's got no chillun at all, and David, he's so good he scarcely touch the ground."

Nick felt a surge of relief. "That's very generous of you, Carry-Ann. And of David, too. You can drive Doc's buggy, because I'm going to stop in town and buy one of my own—if there's one to be had—and also a horse. I can see I'm going to need both, and I might as well go ahead and get them."

Luck was with him. The livery stable man had a buggy that had been left with him for sale, and he promised to keep an eye out for a likely horse that Nick might buy. In the meantime, Nick rented a horse for the day. So it was that Nick followed Doc Pinter's rig along the woodsy road leading to the mine, though he hung back a goodly distance to avoid the reddish dust that curled up from behind Carry's wheels.

About halfway, the rented horse went lame.

Nick pulled over into the shade to find the trouble. It was a deeply embedded stone, and it took a while to get it out of the sore hoof. Even then the gelding limped a bit, so Nick had lost sight of Carry-Ann's vehicle long before he got under way again.

A horse that came galloping past brought him out of a deep study as he jogged along. He watched it round the bend just ahead of him, wondering who was in such a hurry. Then he heard Carry scream.

He flicked the gelding with the buggy whip. The animal picked up its heels, setting the sore hoof so firmly that Nick knew it had been faking in part before. They rounded the bend in a swirl of dust, to see Doc's buggy stopped in the middle of the road.

A square-built shape leaned into the vehicle, trying to pull Carry-Ann from the seat. The little woman was holding on with all her might to the stanchions that supported the canopy. As Nick drew closer, he saw a big fist draw back and hit Carry soundly on the jaw. She dropped limply into the fellow's hands. He hauled her roughly across his saddle and turned his horse toward the woods.

Nick swung his own buggy to cut between the young man and the forest. The whip was in his hand, and the Brockner boy looked up just as the lash cut across his face.

"Put that woman back in that buggy before I cut you to pieces!" Nick growled. So furious was his tone that Hobie obeyed, though the physician was armed with nothing more deadly than a buggy whip. The pistol thrust into the waistband of Hobie's trousers was forgotten as he laid Carry back in the seat from which he had dragged her.

"I don't know why you think you have some

sort of license to abuse people," Nick said as Hobie turned his round, rather stupid face toward the doctor. "But whatever kind you had, I have just revoked it. If I see you bothering anyone—even if I *hear* of this sort of thing again—I'm going to stomp you flat and leave you for the flies. Do you understand me?"

The boy cringed. Something about the bemused expression on his face told Nick that seldom—perhaps never—had he heard anything similar in his life. "My aunt—she don't object," he whined.

Nick gritted his teeth. "I am not your aunt. I do object. If your aunt has anything to say to me, tell her to come and see me."

A furious voice from behind him brought Nick's head around. "And who do you think you are to abuse my nephew?"

An elegant carriage had pulled up behind Nick's rig. The woman sitting in it was almost as angry as Nick himself.

"I am Doctor Nicholas Blasingame," he said icily. "You have come along at just the right time, madam, to see what sort of little games your nephew uses to while away his hours. Yesterday, he assaulted a man who was simply walking down the street of Moreno. Today he has attempted to, I assume, rape that man's wife, who is my friend and my cousins' employee."

"Well, *I* am Augusta Moran," the woman purred in a dangerous voice. "I do not allow my relation to be bullyragged simply for enjoying himself with niggers. That's what they were put on earth for, our amusement. As you would know, if you were a gentleman."

"Then thank God I am not," answered Nick.

"This lady was on her way to attend your own cook, who almost lost her life—perhaps has done so, by now—in childbirth. I hope that besides being inhumane, you are not also ungrateful."

He bowed. Then, seeing that Carry was sitting up again, he nodded toward the mine. Turning his head, he said, "I fear that I may find it necessary to make a Christian of your nephew. Take care that I do not choose to include you in that lessoning." He touched his horse and Carry's with his whip.

Her gasp of fury was lost in the rattle of the buggies, as they departed in a swirl of dust. But Nick, now that he had time to think, felt a bit shamed by his loss of temper.

"I thought I'd cooled down a lot, Carry," he called to the buggy ahead. "I suppose I haven't lost as much steam as I thought I had."

"Thank the Lord for that," came her deep voice back to him. "I'd be out in the woods fighting off that young devil, if you'd took up much time calming down. And he's too big and strong for me. Looks like he's took a dislike to my family. Do you think so? If that's the way it is, we's in a lot of trouble. Black folks can't buck the Morans."

And white folks don't, he thought, though he said nothing. That was the trouble, he felt certain. Money and muscle had combined to create a situation that was frightening and dangerous. Too few of the local people had the nerve to dig in their heels and resist the combination. Until now.

Sheepishly, Nick recognized in himself an eagerness to battle the system he had found here. He had hated leaving Baltimore, not only because of family ties, but because it wasn't like him to run

51

from anything. Only the fact that the situation there was literally unbeatable had made him leave Maryland. Now he had a second chance. He was finding that he reveled in it.

Cool down, old son, he thought. *Getting fighting mad helps sometimes, but when you're in a poker game, it'll lose you your shirt.*

The row of company houses came into view, as they rounded a bend in the crooked road. Nick could see Doc Pinter standing on the porch of the Walds' home. The old man was looking up the road expectantly, and he came to the end of the path to meet the two buggies as they reined to a halt.

"I see you took my advice, Doctor. That is a nice vehicle. I looked at it myself once. I hope you only rented that horse...he's known far and wide as a lazy, good-for-nothing hoof-dragger.

"Carry! You just can't know how happy I am to see you. I have been standing on the porch, concentrating that Mrs. Hazelton would think to send you out here. There's nobody in the country who can or will do a better job of taking care of poor Lucy than you will.

"Come in, Doctor, and see your patient. She looks much better this morning. The fact that the child lived has been as good as a tonic to her. She is determined to make it so she can bring him up."

Nick looped the reins around a post standing beside the road and moved forward to the side of the other buggy. "Carry, are you all right?" he asked, reaching up to take her bundle of spare clothing as she climbed down from the high seat.

"My jaw's sore, but that's all the damage he done me," she answered. "Doc Pinter, you want me to go on in and take a look at Miz Lucy?"

The little man nodded, watching them both with bird-bright eyes. As soon as she had disappeared into the house, he pounced upon nick.

"What happened, Doctor? Something did, I can see that plainly. Carry has a bruise on her cheek and a strange look in her eyes."

Nick glanced toward the porch. Nobody was in sight, but he nodded toward a chinaberry tree that leaned its shade into the dust of the road a short way past the row of houses. "Let's get into the shade out of people's way, and I'll tell you," he said.

Pinter went even paler than usual and he set out for the tree, his short legs making hard work of keeping up with Nick's long ones.

Nick chuckled. "Don't be in such a hurry. Nothing earth-shaking happened. We just had another run-in with that damn Brockner boy. This time he attacked Carry-Ann. He knocked her unconscious and started to carry her into the woods. Luckily, I was only a little distance behind, and I got there in time to stop him. I gave him a good one across the face with the buggy whip, and then I dressed him down. His aunt, worse luck, came along in time to soften the impact. That woman!" Nick almost growled the last two words.

"You had words with Augusta Moran?" Pinter breathed. "You actually disagreed with her? No man has done that since she was fifteen, or so I've been told. She turns those Irish-blue eyes on them, and they just melt into mush, as I have observed for myself."

Nick had been so angry the woman's looks hadn't impinged upon him. Now he thought back.

Now that he considered more coolly, he recalled pansy-blue eyes beneath a wide cream-colored hat. Black curls escaping into fetching tendrils. Skin like honey laced with cream. Probably, if he had met her in any other circumstances, he might have melted, too. Now even the memory of her beauty didn't seem to dull the edge of his fury.

"She may be a raving beauty," he told Pinter, "but anyone who can sit and mouth the same wicked idiocies that helped to bring about the War is so un-intelligent as to be infuriating. People here may think she sits on God's right hand, but to me she is a nit-brained fool."

Pinter laughed aloud. "I've been here for seven years, and all that time I've been waiting for some-one to come who can cope with that woman. Half the problems in the town can be traced back to her or her husband's interests...directly or indirectly. She runs her husband, who runs the sheriff, who, as you have discovered, runs the town ragged. Her whims are our law. One of her whims is money— lots and lots of money. To have her at your throat can be dangerous, Nicholas:"

The two turned and walked slowly back to the house. Neither felt talkative now, and they climbed the steps onto the porch in silence.

"Everything shipshape, Carry?" Nick called.

Her deep voice answered from the small bed-room. "Sho' is, Dr. Nick. You can come in and see your patients, now."

Lucy Wald, drained and exhausted as she was, looked like a different woman from the wreck he had left in Doc's care. Carry had given her a good wash and brush and tied a pink ribbon in her hair.

Her pale-blue German eyes beamed up at Nick from the pillow, as she tried to raise the infant that now slept on her arm.

"Look at him, Doctor! So big he is! So pink now. Is going to be good, yes?"

Nick lifted the child and looked him over. Laying him on the foot of the bed, he examined him carefully. Then, while Carry rewrapped the infant in its swaddlings, he sat in a rickety chair beside the bed and smiled at Lucy.

"He looks fine, Lucy. Now you just get well fast, for he is going to lead you a merry chase. Let me check you over, while Doc and Carry coo over your son. What do you and Hermann plan to name him?"

She smiled timidly. "We think...you do not mind...? We call him Nicholas William. William for Doctor Pinter, who has been so kind."

Straightening the covers, Nick drew a deep breath. "I am honored," he said. "It will be, if you'll believe me, the first child ever named after me. Back home, I did more surgery than deliveries. Thank you."

Pinter entered the room and touched his shoulder, as he stood looking down at Lucy. "I think I'll go home now and get a little sleep before I open the office. I didn't feel I should take the chance of dozing last night, for fear she might hemorrhage. I'll say goodbye for now. It has been a privilege to work with you, Nicholas."

Nick turned. "I might as well come, too. Carry has things in hand, and Hermann will be in when he can get away from the mine. I need to see if I can find a better horse, too. You're right about this one.

He's a faker and a lazybones. I'll trail you in."

The morning was warming up, but the road was so shaded by the dense woods on either hand that they drove in shadow that turned the red dust to purple in the tunnel beneath the overhanging tree-tops. Nick, short of sleep himself, dozed as the horse walked. The sounds of his hooves were muted in the dust that now was deep. Red veils of the stuff rose behind the high wheels of Doc's buggy ahead of him, and Nick wondered if Pinter, too, wasn't asleep, letting his faithful mare set the course for home.

Lulled by the warm quiet, Nick let his head fall forward on his chest. The gelding remained just out of Doc's dust cloud but well within sight of it. Only the complex song of a mockingbird broke the peace of the morning.

The shot came out of the woods on Nick's left, creasing his left shoulder, which was thrust a bit forward, and zipping a long rip into his dark broadcloth coat. The gelding, startled, broke into a gallop, and Nick hauled on the reins to slow the beast to a stop. He was rummaging one-handed in his bag, when the buggy ahead turned sharply and sped back toward him.

Doc Pinter halted his mare wheel-to-wheel with the Blasingame buggy. He scrambled across to sit beside Nick and look at the wound.

"You'll need a couple of stitches in that," he said, pulling a wad of bandages and a bottle of whiskey from his own bag. "Here, let me put a slug of this into that crease and another slug into you. Then we'll pack it, and I'll hitch this nag behind my own buggy. We're not fifteen minutes out of town, if Lizzie picks up her heels."

"It's nothing to get too upset about." Nick turned Doc's bottle up and took a long swig. "I've been wounded worse than this riding through thick woods. I can drive on, I think, without any problem."

"Nonsense!" the little dentist said. "You'll move around and make that thing bleed again. By the time we get to town, if you're careful and stay quiet, it should be crusted over. Don't be silly, boy. Climb into my rig and lean back."

Nick climbed into the rig. He could hear the man fussing about at the rear of the vehicle. Then he climbed in beside Nick and chucked to Lizzie, who swung wide in a turn. As they went about, Nick could see the rented horse following obediently.

"You know, if the angle had been a bit different, or if I had leaned any farther forward, that would have gone directly into my heart beneath my armpit," he said. "I think whoever did that really intended to kill me, not you. You had already passed, and everybody knows your mare and your buggy anyway. There is only one person who might think he has cause to shoot me."

"Brockner," grunted the dentist. "That boy's done everything except murder, since he got big enough to let out alone. His aunt has bought off fathers of raped daughters, owners of stolen horses, husbands of terrified wives. I don't doubt he believes she can buy off the law, even if he kills someone. And she probably can, make no mistake." He frowned.

"Every county is pretty well a law unto itself here. Particularly if you have the governor in your pocket, as the Morans do. You've made a bad enemy."

"There wasn't any way to avoid it," said Nick. "I couldn't have left either David or Carry-Ann to his mercies."

Before Pinter could reply, there came a whirl of dust up ahead. A handsome rig appeared, bowling down the middle of the narrow roadway. The big bays pulling it were being whipped up, and Doc had to pull his mare off into the weeds at the edge of the road to let the carnage pass.

Nick recognized it at once as the same one that had pulled up behind him earlier. Now it held two people, one being Augusta Moran. She held a crimson sunshade over her elegant hat. The other was William Exeter St. John.

Nick straightened as well as he could manage, trying to look entirely well and unwounded. St. John glanced up, then looked back at his companion. As the vehicles passed each other, Augusta's gaze met that of Nicholas Blasingame. Wicked amusement danced in her eyes.

"Now that's a pair to make the devil smile," grunted Pinter as he pulled the mare back into the road. "Did you see the look that hellcat gave you? She knows damned well her nephew tried to pot-shoot you. You can take that as Gospel. And she didn't do a thing to discourage him, either. Bad medicine, Nick. Bad medicine!"

Nick knew those words had nothing to do with his profession.

CHAPTER FIVE

Hoping to avoid a lot of fuss, Nick and Pinter stopped in front of Doc's office and hitched the two buggies, side by side, to the railing. Doc unlocked the front door and swept the two of them into the office before anyone outside had time to observe the blood on Nick's arm.

"Lie down on the cot, and I'll clean that out and patch it up," Pinter said. "I may not know much about regular medicine, but I know just about all there is to know about gunshot wounds. Since I came here, I've attended to thousands of them!"

Nick sank into the combination dentist-barber chair. "This will be fine. And don't think I'm not glad to have you attend to this. You're a much better doctor than you think you are. Alicia told me you became really depressed about practicing since you lost a maternity case, and that's nothing to get you down. We came within an inch of losing that one last night. We just don't know all we should about the process. Nobody I know of is even trying to develop new techniques for dealing with problems in that area. Ouch!"

The last comment came on the heels of Doc's swab. The crease flamed with pain for a long moment. Then the burning dulled to a bearable level, while Doc stitched up the long gash.

"Keep a close eye on that, Nicholas. You don't want to let an infection rob you of the use of that arm. I noticed last night that you use either hand—a convenient talent, that one—but you don't want to lose anything you can keep. There!" Doc wound a final layer of bandage around Nick's shoulder and chest and pinned it neatly over his heart. "That will be easy for you to reach, when you change the dressing. Or you can come to me, if it's convenient.

"Now, why don't you lie down on my cot in the back? It's quite comfortable, and you're right here near your cousins. There's not a bit of use of your going all the way out to their house, when there's nobody there to do for you."

"I'm not all that incapacitated, Doc," Nick replied. "But I think I'll stay here until I feel a bit steadier. It's not so much the wound as it is the whiskey. That has made my head spin. When I've taken a little nap, I think I'll feel like going to look for a decent horse. You go on home and get your rest. You need it."

So Pinter drove away in his buggy, and Nick sank into an uneasy doze on the narrow cot behind a curtain in the back of Pinter's office. He kept waking with a start, hearing again the flat slap of the shot, seeing the look in Augusta Moran's eyes as her carriage passed him. After a time, however, he relaxed and sank into a deep sleep.

He woke to the sound of the office door's bell, which hung from a spring above the moving panel. Pulling back the curtain, he saw Alicia coming toward him with a bowl and a pitcher on the tray she carried.

"Did I wake you? Doc told me what happened, and he said to bring you something to eat in a couple of hours. You go back to sleep, if you'd rather do that than eat."

"Now when did I ever prefer anything at all to eating?" Nick teased, sitting up and stretching as well as he could without hurting himself. "Oof! That's sore! Now what do you have in that bowl? It smells delicious."

She whisked off the white cloth, covering the thick pottery. That revealed steaming soup, thick with meat and vegetables. "Mrs. Flanders always puts a pot of soup on over at the bakery. Since the restaurant closed, most of us who work in town go over there to get our midday meal. You can't beat hot soup and home-made bread for lunch. And she only serves her 'special' to her friends."

Nick pushed aside some books from the small table flanking the cot. Alicia set the tray there and sat on the end of the cot as Nick attacked his lunch.

"Doc wouldn't tell me anything except that you'd been slightly wounded by a stray shot from the woods," she said. "He told me that if you wanted me to know the rest, you'd tell me, but he wouldn't take it upon himself to do it. Now I want to know what happened!" She looked at him expectantly, as he finished off the soup, the last of the warm bread, and a glass of milk.

So Nick told her what the night had held, and of the attack on Carry-Ann, which he didn't gloss over. He knew that Alicia understood only too well what the locals were capable of doing. He concluded, with a sigh, "It seems too much of a coincidence that I should be shot just after that set-to with Brockner and his aunt. If you had seen the look she gave us as she passed us later, you would know that something messy is in the wind."

Alicia nodded, her brow furrowed and her eyes distant with some interior thought. "You don't find her...attractive?" she asked.

He laughed. "Allie, Allie, you're a bright brave girl, but you're a woman to your shoe heels. I knew you were going to ask that. I can say, quite honestly, that I have never seen a woman who was less attractive to me. Taken feature by feature, she should be one to overwhelm the least susceptible. But when you add to her looks her character and philosophy, you get a big fat ugly, as far as I can see."

Alicia nodded again, this time sharply and with conviction. "I should have known my cousin Nick would be immune to her charms. I've been a little worried, ever since you got here, about your reaction to her. Almost every man in town will close his eyes to all sorts of nasty goings-on if she tells them to. The sheriff wouldn't be nearly as bad as he is, just on Tom Moran's say-so. That...witch has him hog-tied."

Nick stood and looked down at his coat. "Do you suppose you could mend this a bit? Just so it won't look so obvious? I need to go and find me a good horse for the buggy."

Alicia took the tray and led the way out of the office, locking the door behind them. Once inside the mercantile, she took needle and thread and made him sit while she stitched the ragged gash in his coat.

"Go and see Mrs. Flanders," she told him when

he was presentable. "Her husband used to have a buggy, but he lost it in a poker game. Now they have an extra horse, and I feel sure they would sell him to you. He has a black gelding, three years old, well trained. He'd be very one for you. He's just eating up their grass now without working for it."

That proved to be the case. Well before closing time, Nick found himself the owner of a handsome black beast that Mrs. Flanders, with unexpected romanticism, had named Lancelot. Once hitched to the new buggy, Lance took up his new duties with enthusiasm. Nick drove around a bit while he waited for Bart and Alicia to finish their work.

He found that the town consisted of three north-and-south streets, parallel to one another. On the central one stood the business area with which he was familiar. Just to the east was the one on which the livery stable stood. To the west a little-used alley held a half-built store, the land office, and the office of Moran Mining Company. One street crossed east-to-west, cornering just beyond Mrs. Flanders's bakery. It made the saloon a corner location.

Beyond the limited confines of the town were lanes along which several houses stood. More houses were being built, and Nick surmised that the mine had brought new people into Moreno. The railroad, too, seemed to be attracting new population.

There was no crowding. His Maryland-oriented eyes opened wide at the farm-sized gardens and orchards that surrounded most of the dwellings. Fields and woods stretched away in all directions once he was past the residential area, and within a mile in any direction, he found himself in the middle of a wilderness.

There was room to breathe here, he realized. Unlike the crowded confines of the East, the new country was spacious and inviting. Though his shoulder began to throb before he again reached the outskirts of town, he was a bit intoxicated with the pine-scented air. Whiffs of blooming plants mingled with the caressing warmth of the sun as he pulled up in front of the mercantile. He hitched his new horse to the railing and stood in the doorway, watching Alicia and Bart lock up for the night.

"I looked around for a while this afternoon," he said, as Alicia went past with an armload of ledgers. "I hadn't realized, even after the train journey, that there was so much room in this part of the world. Do you suppose I could find a place to buy—somewhere near you and Bart, if possible?"

Bart finished securing his iron-shutter grill and turned with a broad smile. "That would be wonderful, Nick. It really would. There's a place right up the road from us, too. It just went on the market a month or so ago. The house isn't finished. Mr. Theodore Pinkston died before he finished it, and his wife and children went back to Mississippi, but you'll be having a lot of people who want to work out their doctor's bills. You can get the rest of the work done without much cash outlay."

"Just be sure it's what you want to do," added Alicia. She had locked her ledgers into the big safe and shut the massive door. "I don't want to over-influence you, but we would so much like you to stay. It probably warps our judgment. I don't want us to warp yours, too.

"We'll look around and see what is available.

You think about it for a while. Then if something comes up that you can't or won't stand for, you won't be anchored here. You can turn your back and leave."

"You sound as if you expect a lot of trouble," Nick said, as the three left and padlocked the door behind t hem. "More than there has already been?"

She sighed. "Nick, my dearest Coz, you haven't seen more than the tip of the iceberg. Even being shot—and you were just lucky it wasn't fatal—hasn't shown you the really dark side of the situation. Not until you are forced to shoot someone yourself will you understand what is going to be asked of you sooner or later.

"I know you too well. You've set your life and your skills toward helping and healing people. Give yourself time to size up the problems here before you commit yourself too deeply."

He handed her up into the buggy beside Bart; then he climbed into his own to follow them homeward. Her words echoed inside him, as he watched the elongated shadow of Lancelot and the buggy precede him eastward.

She's right, he thought. *I've always been slow to anger. The idea of hurting anyone is something I seldom entertain. Can I cope with the sort of things I've already seen happening here?* He glanced at Lancelot and touched him with the whip, for they were falling behind the other vehicle.

Then his doubts subsided. The tough core of stubborn pride that had set him at sword's point with the most influential men in Baltimore prodded him sharply. He laughed a bit wryly.

Aloud, he said, "I've run for the last time. I

couldn't lick the problem in Baltimore. It was too big, and the thing was too entrenched. This time it's different. This is a small situation, though a nasty one. It's more my size. If I have to learn skills that sit oddly on a doctor's shoulders in order to cope with it, then so be it. I'm staying in Moreno. I like the country. I like being near my cousins. I even like...yes, I even like a fight, if it's in a good cause."

The sun was down now, and the buggies reached the Hazelton farm in twilight punctuated by a thousand firefly sparks across the scented fields. This time, Nick insisted on helping with the horses, even though Alicia protested that he should rest his wounded arm.

He managed to prevail, and while he and Bart hung the harness and turned the horses into the small meadow behind the stables, he was thinking how to approach the subject of buying a house once again.

Bart saved him the trouble. "You know, Nick, I think Alicia's wrong, this time. You've had to eat a lot of crow. We got all sorts of letters and clippings from the family, while you were wading into those bastards back home. That's not your style at all.

"Only the fact that they caught you unaware allowed them to get at you as they did. You expected those Baltimore gentlemen to behave like gentlemen, particularly the ones who belonged to our own family. Nobody will ever catch you off guard that way again, if I know you at all. You'll never be satisfied until you clean up somebody's mess, just to prove to yourself that you can. Correct me if I'm wrong."

Blasingame grunted. He hadn't suspected Bart,

whom he halfway considered to be still a boy, to understand him so well.

He chuckled. "You're right, you know. I was mulling it over as we drove out. I want to buy a place here. I want to put down my roots and dig in and help those who need helping and stand toe to toe with those who need horsewhipping. I'll never feel right if I don't."

Bart laughed aloud. "That's what I thought! Now come in to dinner before Al skins us both."

As they lingered over coffee after dinner, Nick out lined his plans to Alicia. She accepted his reasoning, though he could tell by her expression that she would never understand his motivations—not completely, at least. Still she nodded at last and rose to clear the table. Nick stacked the plates as she took them away.

She took a pile from him and said, "If you want a house, we'll find you a house. And land. You'll want a few head of cattle, and you will accumulate pigs and chickens so fast that you won't believe it. Your patients will pay you in livestock and produce. You have to have a farm in sheer self defense. A farm or else a large family of hungry children." She laughed wickedly. "I expect you to come up with those, too, of course.

"Tomorrow we'll close early and run out to the Pinkston place. It would be perfect, and I know you can get it reasonably. Mrs. Pinkston left the selling of the place to Oren Robertson at the land office. He's a good old man, honest as they day is long. Not too bright, you understand, but you can depend on him."

"He's so dumb and so honest," Bart broke in,

67

"That he's never caught on to the fact that Tolliver and Whitfield and the Morans are a bunch of crooks. Augusta goes in to visit him about once a month to keep him totally bemused with her looks. And then Tom gets the city officials to slide some piece of crookedness right past his eyes, while he's too dazzled to see."

"That's unkind!" protested Alicia. However, she didn't deny the truth of his words.

So it was that the next afternoon found them on their way past the Hazelton home on their way to look at the house. Nick had pleaded his wound to get Doc to take one more day of medical problems onto his shoulders, but he knew he must set up his own office soon.

That didn't worry him as they rode along the shaded road, however. The day had been over-warm, but as the sun declined, a coolness breathed out of the forest. Nick found himself refreshed and enthusiastic.

They pulled into a long drive that curved toward a two-story house of some size. Young pecan trees had been planted on either side of the approach, and Nick could envision the stately avenue they would eventually become. Cleared meadows lay on either hand, though he could see deep forest beyond them. That swept around to come within a hundred yards of the back of the house, he found.

They hitched Lance to an iron post sporting a lantern hook, and Nick helped Alicia down, while Bart charged ahead with the keys that Robertson had given them. By the time they came up to him, he had the heavy double-leaved door open.

They stepped into the high-ceiled hall beyond it.

A stair angled upward at the back of the huge entry hall, which, like Alicia's, was of a size to form a sitting room. The rooms on either hand were large and airy, their many-paned windows shuttered with louvers on the inside against the hot sun of summer.

Once Bart showed him the dimensions of the farm that went with the house, Nick was sold on it. A hundred acres was all he would ever have time to care for, yet it would be ample for any livestock he might acquire in the practice of his profession. It lay on the eastern curve of a rolling hill, falling away to a low meadow, well watered with springs that ran away to a deep cut feeding into the river. The woods comprised three-fourths of the place, assuring an ample supply of firewood as well as of timber for building.

"There isn't any use in looking at anything else," said Nick. "I like the house. I like the land. Any more looking would only confuse me. I'll talk to Robertson tomorrow."

Yet that didn't happen. As soon as they reached town the next day, a rider came after Nick. Hermann Wald had a badly injured man at the mine, and the services of both Blasingame and Doc Pinter were needed. They went out together in Nick's new buggy, and the physician took the opportunity to tell the little dentist of his plans for buying a farm.

Pinter squinted down his pudgy nose. "Just spoiling for a fight, aren't you, young Nicholas?" he asked. "The Morans have already passed the word. Nobody is to sell you anything or to call you when they're sick. They'll be mightily upset when they find you've been out to the mine, but Hermann isn't about to lose a man just to please the Morans." He chuckled.

"He's the only qualified mine foreman in East Texas, and they know it as well as he does. He'll call you when he thinks he needs you. And you'll go. Most of the time you'll treat the people out there for nothing, which is just about what they've got. Most aren't even independent enough to try to do some work for you to pay you for your time. Except for Hermann, of course. That's a good man, there.

"Anyway, if you stay here, you're in for a fight and a half. They've got St. John here for some sort of chicanery. I can feel that in my bones. And he, my friend, is not your garden-variety crook like Tolliver. Nor is he a feeble-minded troublemaker like Hobie Brockner. He's A-Number-One trouble."

Pinter grinned up at Nick. "I can see that I'm scaring you out of your wits," he chuckled. "You don't give a bit more of a damn or have any more judgment than I did at your age. Tackle a tiger, I would, and give it the first two bites. I will venture to give you a word of advice—watch land-selling transactions."

Nick stared at him questioningly.

"There's a lot of interest in Texas land right now up in the East and the North. There has been a flurry of interest here, in fact. That makes an ideal set-up for a swindle, if you have the stomach for that sort of thing. And that is where I think the Morans are focusing their attention. St. John would be an ideal front man, wouldn't he? All that British culture just oozing out of him. Fool anybody just about. You watch anyway. Particularly, you watch St. John."

Nick stared up the tree-shaded road. It made sense. St. John was not the sort to rob banks or hold up trains. Something more smooth and sophisticated was more in his line—like selling land he had no right to sell? Or swamps to unsuspecting buyers?

He nodded. "Thank you, Doc. You're a sharp man, and I'm glad you're on my side."

They pulled up at the mine gate and called. A man came running from a shed inside the fence and unlocked the gate.

"Glad to see you, sirs. Old Ham, he's hurt bad. Go right past the tool house there and pull up in back of it. They've got him there."

Nick whipped up Lancelot. All thought of the peculiar problems of Moreno faded into the back of his mind.

A patient was waiting.

CHAPTER SIX

It was a long morning. Old Ham had caught his arm in the pulley system, and relentless gears had drawn his shoulder and part of his torso into it before his mates could shut off the steam-powered system. The arm was gone. The greatest surgeon in Christendom could not have saved that mangled mess. Nick did his best to save as much as possible, however, hoping to attach a hook or something of the sort later. It would give the man some sort of use of the remnant, he thought.

"He should go into a hospital right now," the physician said, as he washed his bloody hands and rolled down his sleeves. "The shock and loss of blood could kill him, not to mention internal injuries I may not have caught in the midst of the general mess."

"Would that we had one," said Pinter, handing him his coat. "Many a life could be saved, if we did.

"The previous doctor had a sort of nursing home where he could keep those patients who needed close attention. When he died, it was closed, and some years ago it burned down. That might be a crusade for you, if you need another one. Convince the Morans that their civic duty requires them to supply a hospital—for the people who are all but killed by their cheap-jack machinery." He glared at the bucket-and-pulley system, which was working away as if it had never tasted blood.

"As it is, he's luckier than most. His mama is a wise old woman. She'll take fine care of him or make his sister do it while she oversees the job. Old Ma'am is too stove up with rheumatism to get around much herself, but she'll have Ham's wife and sister and daughters stepping lively. She's nursed everything from tuberculosis to alligator bites. Just tell her what must be done, and she'll see to it. You can bank on that."

Ham was laid in a wagon, which bore him to his own door. The wails of his womenfolk were hushed with stem vigor by the wizened old woman who supervised those carrying her son into the house. She saw him placed on a low bed in the front room. Then she went out to wait for Nick to finish his survey of the bandages for a last time.

Blasingame simplified his instructions, knowing that his nurse was illiterate. To his astonishment, a glimmer in her eyes told him she knew very well what he was doing, and it was completely unnecessary. But by then it was too late to change tactics. He finished up a bit wryly, bade the family goodbye, and walked up the road toward the Walds'.

Pinter had gone ahead, and Nick saw the little dentist waiting in the shade of the tree under which they had talked before. They walked on together, to find Carry-Ann waiting on the porch for their arrival.

"Miz Lucy, she says I'm to go on home with you all, Dr. Nick. She say she feeling mighty- nigh well. Her neighbor's going to tend to things for her until she can get around. I know she ain't as chirpy as she makes out, but she feels beholden. I thinks she'll do right well. Mr. Hermann's a mighty good hand to take hold around the house. That's a good man. Anyway, I 'spect Miz Alicia will be gad to see me traipse home again."

"How's the bleeding?" Nick asked her. They went into the little bedroom and greeted Lucy Wald.

"Done quit. She's healing up faster than scat. Don't know how you done it, Doctor. I changed the dressings this morning, and there wasn't hardly nothing on 'em." Carry leaned to touch the sleeping baby's head very gently. "I'm going to miss little Nicholas. He the sweetest baby. Just eats and sleeps and looks round at everybody like he was growed up already."

He found that Lucy was indeed mending fast. Her stout German constitution stood her in good stead. She was in surprisingly good condition, considering the major surgery she had undergone. He cautioned her repeatedly about trying to get up too soon, however.

"Take a month, Mrs. Wald. You need it, believe me. You have good neighbors and a helpful husband—it's possible for you. I'll be back as soon as I can to see you and Old Ham. I expect to see you right there in that bed." He fixed her with a stern eye, and she blushed.

"My Mama, she would have baby in the morning and do big wash in afternoon!" she protested.

"But you didn't just have a baby. You lost a good-sized chunk of yourself, and you're stitched together like a crazy-quilt. You start moving around, bending over, and you're going to rip out all my careful stitches. Then who'll raise little Nick? I can't have my godson lacking a mother."

Her blush deepened. "You mean this?" You will be his godfather? We would be so grateful, Doctor!"

Nick grinned, chucked the child gently under his multiple chins, and followed Doc and Carry-Ann out into the front yard. The obliging neighbor was waiting to speak with him. He found her fairly bright, and she seemed to understand his instructions well. He left both his patients, to his relief, in what seemed capable hands.

He turned to Carry-Ann. "Would you mind driving into town? I'd like to ride in back with Doc. My shoulder's twinging like mad. I should take a bit of my own advice about moving around too much after being stitched up."

She climbed into the buggy and flipped the reins expertly against Lance's back. He started off toward town, as Nick leaned back in the small seat in the rear of his buggy. It wasn't meant for reclining, he found, and he sighed.

Doc looked at him sternly. "I knew you were doing too much," he said.

"So did I," said Nick. "But you go when you're needed. Didn't you always do that?"

"*Touché*. But I must admit that I never went with a bullet crease in me."

"Doc, I'm worried," Nick said very softly, so Carry-Ann wouldn't hear. "That attack on Alicia—even if she did give better than she got—that scares me. Bart is the best boy in the world, but he never was what you might call aggressive. I wonder if he can handle the situation in Moreno on a long-term basis. He always was polite and well-spoken, and my grandmother loved him dearly, but I wouldn't have picked him to be the one to protect my cousin and her child. Not in the sort of circumstances I can see coming up. He's too...easy-going, I suppose you'd call it."

Doc spat over the rear wheel, cleared his throat, and leaned toward Nick. "You've not been here very long." he observed, his tone quiet. "Things have been happening all along since your cousins arrived. It took them a bit to realize what was happening, for they didn't expect it. When they understood, they took steps. For the most part, they've stymied the crooks in town pretty thoroughly.

"I got there just after Alicia shot that deputy. If I ever saw a man ready to kill, it was her husband. I think he'll handle himself well, if the time comes when he has to. Easygoing people are sometimes the most ferocious, when you threaten those they love."

Nick nodded, not entirely satisfied. As he closed his eyes against the glare of noon, he saw again in his memory the sweet-tempered lad who had followed his much-older friend with puppy-like fidelity. That boy hadn't had much fierceness in him, Nick was certain. But the memory was lost in a doze that ended only with their arrival in Moreno.

He was feverish again. Alicia spotted it at once.

"You go home, right now, with Carry-Ann. We'll check with Robertson about the Pinkston place, if you want us to. You need to be in bed, not running around the country taking care of the Morans' problems."

"I will, I will, I promise!" Nick laughed. "But I truly do need to check on office space. I thought about subletting part of Doc's office space, and then I realized that would crowd both of us. I want to get the empty space right next door to him, just across the street from you. Then I can use what space I need and possibly sublet what I don't require."

His cousin agreed with some reluctance, and Nick went with Doc to the lawyer's office above Mrs. Flanders' bakery. Ernest Hunt, Attorney-at-Law, as his door sign announced, was a short, fat creature the color of a slug. Nick had a moment's uneasiness—the man looked so shady that the physician thought he surely must be in the pockets of the Moran interests. However, he seemed cordial.

"Doctor Blasingame, happy to meet you, sir. We have needed another doctor here since the mine began operating. Most happy! Most happy! And you want the space next to Doctor Pinter? That property is a bit run-down. I can make you a good price on its rental or lease, if you agree to do the cleanup yourself. You probably will want to make some alterations and additions suitable to your needs, anyway. No need to clean it up when workmen will just mess it right up again, is there?"

Doc winked at Nick behind the pudgy back. Nick smiled amiably at the lawyer. "It sounds like good thinking to me. There seems to be plenty of room. Would there be any objection if I decide to sublease part of it, if there turns out to be more than I need?"

"Not at all. Not at all. I'm only happy to get the space occupied. An empty building detracts from the look of a town, don't you agree? Puts off prospective businesses and buyers, you know. That will fill all the existing spaces along Main Street and *that,* sir, will be good for the town."

Nick recognized a typical town booster. He had met many of that type. They had their gazes fixed firmly upon some point in the invisible middle distance of the future, at which they believed that a utopian state of total prosperity would be achieved, if only they kept the faith and remained determined.

"I hope to live in Moreno for a long time to come perhaps for the rest of my life, "he told the man. "I hope that my coming will benefit the town. Will you prepare the necessary papers? And inform me as to the amount, of rent I will be paying?"

In a few minutes everything was in order. Nick and Doc left Hunt busily scribbling on sheaves of paper. As they reached the foot of the precipitous stairway leading down to the street, Doc paused and held up a warning hand. Nick leaned to look down over Pinter's shoulder.

A young woman had been making her way down the boarded walkway, her arms filled with packages. The bundles now lay helter-skelter about her feet, as she struggled in the grip of a grinning young man. His obvious intention of kissing her was interrupted by her determined efforts to free her hands. The one she loosed she immediately balled into a fist and popped into his right eye. He lost his grip and stepped backward.

This all took place before Doc or Nick could move to assist her. Now they hurried down to help her retrieve her packages. Her assailant saw them coming and retreated across the street into the sheriff's office. That gave Nick a good idea who he might be.

"Another deputy?" he asked. He secured the

loosened string around a parcel and handed it to her.

She looked up, and he got his first real impression of her. She was no beauty of the Augusta Moran type, but she had an oval face, tanned to golden cream, that was lighted by an extraordinary pair of intelligent black eyes. Her dark coil of hair had been loosed in the struggle and looped beneath the frill of a dimity bonnet. All in all, she made the most fetching picture Nick had seen since Baltimore.

Before she could reply, Doc said, "Do forgive me, Miss Ellen. I am remiss. This is Doctor Nicholas Blasingame, the Hazeltons' cousin from the East. And this, Nick, is Ellen Harper, who is our schoolmistress. Her mother's people were the original Morenos, who settled here before 1820. Her father was the doctor I told you about—the one who had the nursing home."

Nick bowed, and Ellen inclined her head. "Thank you for coming to my rescue, Doctors. And yes, that was a deputy. Evidently you have been in Moreno long enough to learn how things are run here, now." There was a dry note in her husky voice that hinted that things had been operated far more smoothly in her grandfather's era.

"Have you far to walk?" asked Nick. "I am about to be sent home by my cousin Alicia. Carry-Ann is driving my carriage. Could I take you home, with all your burdens?"

"That would be lovely." Ellen smiled. "I must admit that I'm a bit shaken up. I am not used to being attacked at midday on the public street. Might I wait for you at the mercantile?"

It was arranged, and Nick soon found himself

sitting behind Carry-Ann and Ellen Harper and finding the view admirable. She half-turned in the seat to talk with him, and he found that her face in three-quarters was quite as taking as it had been full-on.

"I heard that you had been shot," she said, her tone concerned. "Surely it could not have been a serious wound, or you wouldn't be about so soon."

"No, I'm not all that brave and stoic," Nick agreed. "It was just a crease, but after working all morning at the mine with an injured man, I find I'm a bit feverish. Alicia all but put me across her knee for going out there at all. She told Carry-Ann to keep me quiet this afternoon, if she has to tie me up and nail my shoes to the floor. Didn't she, Carry-Ann?"

"She did. Told me to make chicken broth and see he eats it, if I has to hold him down and pour it in. Then to pull his blinds down and make him take a nap. She'll skin us both, if he goes gallivanting around any more today. If it hadn't been you, Miz Ellen, she'd never have let us go out of our way even the little bit to take you home."

He chuckled. "Now that I have met you, I would certainly like to do a very modest bit of gallivanting, too. Would you object if I called upon you some evening, if there comes one that I can call my own?" he asked her.

Ellen's dark eyes looked serious as she said, "I must tell you, Doctor, that even though my mother's family was one of the finest in Spain, those who are in the ascendant here now consider me a 'dirty greaser.' You might well compromise your own standing in the community by making a friend of me. But I would welcome a visit from you at any time. My grandmother will be charmed to meet you. I must admit there are very few people here now with whom I can carry on a literate conversation."

"I'll brush up my literacy," Nick said, his tone solemn, though his eyes were dancing. "And I find that social standing is a thing that irks me terribly. Besides which, if one ostracizes the would-be ostracizers before they can get in the first lick, the battle is won. Then they stumble over one another trying to get your attention. They forget they ever intended to look down on you, because you're looking down on them. Or they think so, which comes out to the same thing."

Ellen's husky chuckle was a delight. "I shall remember that," she said, as the vehicle pulled up before a rambling frame house whose curving porch was dripping with purple wisteria. She would not allow Nick to get down and help her into the house with her packages.

"Do not, I beg, get me into hot water with your cousin. She is the only civilized acquaintance I can claim. My pupils, bless them, are far from being semi-civilized, at this point. You might like to meet them, Doctor. They would be terribly impressed to have a learned Eastern physician visit them at school. It would be a good thing, don't you think, if we could get one interested in becoming a doctor himself? Or so it seems to me. For future reference?"

"I'll be glad to visit your school," Nick said, as she turned to go up the path toward the porch. "Name the day, and I'll be there. I'll even pull the skeleton out of my trunk and put it together. That should get their attention."

"Perfect," she laughed. Then she was gone.

Nick sank back into his uncomfortable seat. "Carry, remind me to get somebody to put a comfortable sitting place back here. It seems that I spend most of my time n the back of my own buggy. I wouldn't wish this Iron Maiden on my worst enemy."

She laughed, clucking to Lancelot. He wheeled smartly and took out for home. Once they arrived, Nick found his nurse adamant. He must drink the broth she made in an incredibly short time from a chicken Alicia had dressed that morning. Then he must lie in his darkened room and sleep.

He found he couldn't manage that. The small amount of fever in him sent odd pictures spinning through his mind. He lay in a semi-daze, watching patterns of red and purple and orange coalesce on the insides of his eyelids. The worry about Alicia's position in the Moreno situation underlay all the nonsense, and he found himself, at last, watching helplessly as the deputy attacked his cousin. The sound of hr shot woke him from his stupor, and he found it had been the front door, which had blown shut in the draft.

The sun was well down over the western trees. He propped the door open again with the china dog doorstop. He could smell supper cooking in the kitchen. When he investigated, he smiled at Carry-Ann and asked, "They should be home pretty soon, shouldn't they?"

Her bright chignon bobbed with her nod. "I 'spects 'em right now," she said. "Sometimes, though, they gets late customers, and then I just leaves things in the warming oven for 'em. David comes in so tired, I hates for him to have to get his own grub. He'll be surprised to see me home this evening. He didn't expect me till tomorrow."

Nick stepped onto the wide veranda and looked up the road. The evening shadows were stretched across it, and the mingled scents of a thousand different blooming things enchanted the evening. A few late jonquils bloomed by the porch, and he walked down the pathway to get a better look at the flowering quince beside the road.

The hot day had become a heavenly evening. He ambled easily up the road, thinking to meet the wagon. A whippoorwill was calling in the woods, and peepers and tree frogs and thousands of crickets were tuning up all around him. A sense of well-being washed away the fever of the afternoon. He stepped out toward Moreno, feeling that he could walk the entire way, if need be.

A jangle of harness and the rattle of hardware interrupted his mellow mood. He shaded his eyes against the last of the sun and looked up the purple-shadowed road.

Bart's rig was coming full-tilt toward him. The bays were running dead-out, their nostrils distended, their mouths dripping foam. Alicia was driving, and when he saw her face, his heart dropped toward his boots.

His cousin was both furious and frightened, and nowadays it took a lot to frighten her. He could see no sign of Bart.

CHAPTER SEVEN

She was holding back on the reins, slowing the bays in order to swing into the drive without upsetting the carriage. As she passed her cousin, she shouted to him.

"Hurry, Nick! Bart's down the road, and he needs help! Get your bag, while I load the guns!" The last was called over her shoulder as she whirled into the drive, leaving him standing in a cloud of dust.

Amid the peace of the. evening, it was shocking to have such a demand come rocketing out of the blue. Nick, however, sped after the vehicle, cut across the lawn to the front door, and entered the house almost on Alicia's heels.

She was already talking to Carry-Ann. "Carry, a bunch of men down the road seem to be stealing Isaiah Crow's cattle, his young stuff that he keeps in the Niño Creek pasture. Get the guns out of the cabinet, while I get the ammunition. Bart's back there with nothing but his pocket pistol. He's going to try to hold them until we can get back to help."

Carry nodded once, her expression inscrutable, and skittered into the bedroom opposite Nick's. As Nick came from his own room, bag in hand, Alicia and Carry were bundling two rifles and a shotgun into the buggy. He hurried to help them, noting with concern that Alicia's fair cheeks were mottled. Her breath seemed to be coming short as well.

"Allie, why don't you let me see about this? You don't need this sort of thing—not right now," he said as she clambered up into the seat before he could move to help her.

"You don't understand," she panted. "There are at least six of them, and they'd kill you and Bart without thinking about it. Three stand a better chance, particularly if I'm one of them. Killing me would set the bees buzzing around their ears, believe me. I know what I'm talking about. Now come on!"

Before he could think, Nick was beside her on the seat, and she had cramped the rig around, whipped out of the drive into the dirt track that was their road, and was flying back the way she had come.

"How far?" he shouted above the flutter of wind in his ears and the clatter of hooves.

"About a mile and a half. There's a creek-bottom pasture separated from the road by an arm of pine woods. We never would have known anything was going on except for the cows bawling. Bart slipped through the trees, saw what was happening, and sent me on for help.

"We were talking to Isaiah just today. He was going to sell those heifers next week and has a buyer all ready to take them. He wanted to bank the money for young Isaiah's education." She didn't look around, and her profile was one that in no way could be identified as that of the proper Miss

Blasingame who had graduated from Miss Atherton's.

They covered the ground in a surprisingly short time, and Alicia pulled the horses to a walk before they reached their destination. She turned into a track that seemed to wander away into the wilderness. There she looped the lines around the whip socket and turned to Nick.

"Bart's about a hundred yards off to the right. I don't hear anything, so he hasn't made himself known yet. He told me to hide behind the biggest tree I could find and provide covering fire. You take the shotgun and rifle to him. He'll want the scattergun. He claims that's the only way to kill snakes. If you can bring yourself to use a gun, we need you. Now go!"

His head whirling, Nick found himself stumbling carefully through heavy growth, burdened with the long guns and several boxes of shells and cartridges. A month ago, if someone had told him that he would be about to engage in a shoot-out with law officers who were thieves, he would have laughed himself silly.

He paused to listen intently. Now he heard clearly the bawling of cows, mingled with shouts, though both were somewhat muffled by the intervening forest. He hissed between his teeth, hoping to catch Bart's attention. Then, fearing the sound wouldn't carry well enough, he called softly, "Bart! Bart! Are you there? It's Nick. I've got the weapons."

There was no reply. He forged ahead through the wood, which was already dark, though the sky above the interlocked branches was still faintly alight with sunset. As he stumbled into stump holes and through brier vines, he heard something ahead of him,

A dark shape loomed up, and Bart whispered, "Here. For God's sake, be quiet. They're almost ready to drive the herd out onto the road. They've been waiting for dark. Follow me!"

Nick silently passed the shotgun and a box of shells to Bart, checked the load of the Winchester repeater that he held, and tried his best to move quietly after his cousin. The trees grew thinner, letting in a bit of light. After the darkness of the thicker forest, it gave pretty good visibility.

Bart led him to a wide clearing that sloped gradually downward from the forest—evidently toward a big creek. The cattle were bunched in an uneasy huddle, and six shadowy figures moved their mounts about, heading in any who tried to bolt.

"You ready?" breathed Bart.

Nick saw his eyes, bright in the dim light. "Ready as I'll ever be," he answered.

Bart stepped from behind the tree that had sheltered them and aimed the shotgun upward and slightly toward the bunched cattle, which were less than fifty yards away. The boom of the ten-gauge echoed round and round the clearing. The heifers threw up their heads and their tails and bolted in all directions.

Without waiting, Bart yelled, "Get them, men! Get the cattle-stealing bastards! I know who they are, every one of them! Halt, you there! You're surrounded, and you'd better give up without a fight!"

The dim shapes wheeled their mounts with one accord and rode for the forest that angled behind them. A single rifle shot slapped flatly, and the flame of the discharge could be seen clearly in the hem of the wood. Alicia had proved to them that they were, indeed, surrounded.

They needed no second reminder. They headed up the pale sand of the trail along which they had intended to drive the stolen heifers. Bart sent another shotgun blast after them.

When the frantic clatter had died away, the two men leaned against a tree and breathed deeply for a moment or two. "Thank God I didn't have to shoot anybody," Nick sighed. "I was ready to, I think, but I didn't enjoy the prospect."

"I know just how you feel," said Bart. "This time we didn't have to spill any blood. But, Nick, unless I'm way out in my calculations, we ought to have killed them all. We'll live to be sorry we didn't, just mark my words. Our worst handicap is the fact that we're not like them. They wouldn't have thought twice about killing us, if things had been reversed."

He broke his shotgun and ejected the spent shell. "Now we'd better see after Alicia. She'd have worried herself sick, if I'd made her stay at the house. This way she knows what happened, and she wasn't in the line of fire." He sighed warily. "I don't want to have to be faced with this kind of thing again. Particularly not with the baby coming."

They cut straight across toward the spot where they had seen the flame from the rifle. The sky was dark now, and the grass across which they walked was a muted gray. Left to himself, Nick would have wandered around in circles all night, he knew, looking for the way home. Bart seemed perfectly oriented.

"You left the carriage in the track?" he asked.

Alicia emerged from the other edge of the wood and came toward them. "Yes. It's not far, if we cut back the way I came. I forgot to bring the lantern.

It seemed a weird journey to Nick. His cousins moved through the thick old forest with a certainty that stunned him. It was as if they had been reared in the wood instead of in the staid old city he knew. Before he could believe it, they had covered the distance to the rig. There they lit the lantern, and in its warm glow he looked at the two with new respect.

"Grandmother would never know you," he said. "She'd be proud of you, make no mistake, but she would find it as hard as I do to believe that you are Bart and Allie...at least, the pair she knew. Have you taken a course in being Indians?"

Allie's laugh was a bit hysterical as Bart lifted her into the vehicle. "We almost bought this place from Isaiah," she said. "We walked it out more than once, before we decided to buy the place we did. We finally decided that this ought to stay in the family for little Ike, so we...loaned Mr. Crow some money so he wouldn't have to sell it."

Nick settled beside her, as Bart backed the horses carefully to a wider spot and turned their heads toward home. "My dears," the doctor said, "you most certainly do not belong in Baltimore. Our trading ancestors would disown you...why, you were supposed to find a man who needs money, then screw him down to the last dime he'll take! Never to lend him enough so he won't be forced to sell to you!" He laughed bitterly. "That's one reason I went into medicine. I'm not expected to cheat my patients."

A thought hit him, and he straightened in the seat. "Do you think those men knew who we were? They couldn't see us. What do you think, Bart?"

"They couldn't recognize my yell, because I never yell," Hazelton answered. "They might put two and two together—who lives out this way and might have been passing at a time to learn what they were doing—but they can't know for certain. Thank God." He looked sideways at Allie, then at Nick. "They're not above threatening women and even children."

The darkness rolled past on either hand, and in a short time a distant light marked the lamp Carry-Ann had left on the porch to light their way home. They were silent as they tended the team, washed up, and ate the meal that had remained warm in Carry-Ann's oven.

Now Alicia was looking pale. The furrows of anger had not left her face.

Bart looked across the table at Nick. His expression serious, he said, "There's going to be an election in a couple of months. I'm running for mayor, against Moran. I know it's foolish and risky. Al has explained every drawback to me in detail. But if I straighten out this mess of a town, it's easier from the top than from the bottom. Given an honest chance, I can win?"

"If you don't get killed in the meantime:" Alicia said. "The Morans may well frame you for something. Nick knows how that feels. And if you could assure the poor, mistreated people who'd vote for you that some gun-carrying deputy wouldn't go right into the polling place and help them to vote...his way...it might work. But elections here have never done anything except what the Tollivers, the Whitfields, and the Morans want done. You know it. Doc has explained it. I want our son to have a father, not a picture on the wall and an obituary notice."

Nick looked at Bart with new respect. If he had considered it, that would have been the tack he would have taken, given the circumstances.

"I'd run, myself, if I had lived here long enough to be qualified," he said. "As it is, I'll just have to take on the task of managing your campaign. It's not as easy to bully two men as it is one. I have a feeling that Pinter will join us. He couldn't do a thing alone, but he's on our side. I know that."

Alicia caught her breath. "In all the excitement, I forgot to tell you. Bart saw Mr. Robertson, and we put down earnest money on the Pinkston place. He said he had full power of attorney, and nothing would have to be sent to Mississippi for Mrs. Pinkston to sign. You're to come by the first chance you have to sign some papers. I think Mr. Robertson is less enchanted by Gussie Moran than he used to be, don't you, Bart?"

Hazelton nodded. "He told me Tom had ordered him not to sell me a place, no matter what or where. He was angry about that, I could see. He said that he had a responsibility to Ted Pinkston's family, and no Irish newcomer was going to tell him he couldn't perform that duty according to his conscience."

They all laughed, the tension easing. "Maybe he has waked up a bit, after all," Alicia said, as she rose to clear the table. Both men got up to help her, but before a hand could be laid to a dish, she turned paper-white and her knees went out from under her. Bart lifted her from the floor, his face as pale as hers.

"Take her into your room," Nick ordered. "Make some hot tea—*very* hot tea—and lace it with whiskey and sugar. I'll get my bag and look her over. I imagine it's mainly excitement and fatigue. Don't look so frightened, man. She's a lot tougher than you think." But when he bent over his cousin, while Bart was in the kitchen firing up the cook stove to warm the water, he felt worried himself. As he touched her temple, Alicia's eyes opened, and she frowned.

"What a fuss! I'm perfectly fine, Nick. I just got overexcited, I think. And my supper didn't sit very well either. I'll be all right tomorrow."

"Of course," he agreed. "But for now, I'm going to give you some hot tea and a pill. You'll sleep like a baby, and tomorrow you will stay right here with Carry-Ann and rest. If there's not too much for me to do, I'll help Bart with the store. You want to ease up a bit. Take care of yourself and your child."

She shook her head doubtfully as Bart bustled back in with the tea. When he heard Nick's advice, he agreed completely.

"I worry about you, Al," he told his wife. "I think that's exactly what you should do. You don't know how you looked this evening. If I had looked that way, you'd have had me in bed before supper. Do it for me. Nick and I can take care of anything that comes up. And tomorrow's Saturday. If things get too hectic, I'll ask Miss Harper to come in and help me. She said I could call on her at any time."

With some difficulty, they convinced her. The

next morning found their two rigs on the road toward Moreno. As they neared the track where Alicia
had hidden the buggy the night before, Bart pulled
up.

"I'd like to check on those heifers," he called to
Nick, who was just behind him. "The Crows don't
have much, and I wouldn't want them to lose any of
it. You mind if I step through the woods to see if I
can spot the animals?"

"Why don't we pull the buggies into the woods
and go together?" asked Nick. "I'd like to see the
field of battle by day, myself."

The wood was filled with a mist of young green.
Dogwoods shimmered in unreal splendor, as the sun
filtered shafts of light through the branches overhead. The scent was intoxicating. Bart pointed out
looping vines of yellow jasmine linking tree to tree,
but there were subtler and more intriguing scents
even than that in the morning air. Nick found himself enjoying the morning walk with acute pleasure.

Too soon, they found themselves at the pasture
clearing. They stepped out into the hoof-marked
track, on which their foes of the night had fled. A
quarter-mile away, across the full width of the flat,
creek-bottom meadow, a group of cattle stood knee
deep in grass, grazing peacefully. There was no sign
of their terror of the night before.

"I think Isaiah ought to round 'em up today and
put the whole bunch in the public pen in town. Once
they're signed in there, the whole town will know
what's happening, if they should disappear. I don't
think even Tolliver could stand having the name of
cattle thief pinned onto him so obviously.

"Once Isaiah has that money safely in the bank

at San Pablo, there's nothing Tolliver and his crew can do about it."

"Do you mean that you can't trust the *bankers* here?" asked Nick. Then he recalled Carry-Ann's tale about her aunt and the teller who had been dissatisfied until her last two dollars had been accounted for. He looked around the meadow with the early sun slanting across its lush expanse.

"...Every prospect pleases, and only Man is vile," he quoted in answer to his own query. "Somehow I had the feeling that if I could get away from the East things would be different. More open and honest. Less...civilized!" he made the term an epithet.

"Not likely," Bart said, turning up the track to follow the hoof marks. "We seem to bring all the blessings of civilization right along with us, no matter where we go. The honest people want to tend to their own business and stay out of trouble. That gives the dishonest—and worse ones—free rein.

"They tell me that a few years ago, before Moreno became more Anglo than Spanish, it was a pretty nice little place. No paradise, of course. What place is? But not anything like the pesthole it is now. And do you know what? I honestly believe that a dirty white man is about ten times dirtier than a dirty anything else. There's something sort of wild and woodsy about an Indian or a black, but a dirty white just stinks."

"Now what brought that on?" laughed Nick.

Bart laughed in turn. "Oh, I guess it was that filthy rascal who came in just before closing last night. If a skunk had followed him into the store, you couldn't have told the difference. Allie turned pale and excused herself. I heard her throwing up in a box in the storeroom, while I waited on him. I almost had to join her.

"He bought a bunch of stuff, too. Crowbars and wire cutters and hacksaws. Paid in cash, which seemed strange because he looked as if he would have been put to it to dig up a dime. In a normal town, I'd have reported the whole transaction to the sheriff after he'd gone."

Nick looked at Bart/ "The sheriff!" they said in unison and broke into a run.

They turned their vehicles toward town and whipped up the horses. Bart's bays could outpace Nick's single black, but he managed to keep the faster buggy in sight. They pulled into the main street, instead of turning toward the stable. Nick pulled up behind Bart's rig, and they jumped down to stand before the mercantile.

The front door stood open. The glass of the big window had been shattered, and the iron grill had been broken into bits. "Thank God Allie stayed home!" Bart said. "This would have given her a terrible setback after last night." He turned to look toward the sheriff's office, and a face was swiftly withdrawn from the window.

"Let's go in and see what's missing. I hate to think what this is going to cost us, but we've been doing very well. There's quite a bit in the San Pablo bank, if we need it. Come on, Nick. I'm glad you're here. Makes me feel better somehow."

Nick managed a strained smile. "I'm glad of that, anyway," he said. Together, they stepped into the store. It was a shambles. Counters had been split, their glass pulverized. It was impossible to estimate what stock was missing, for it was mixed together on the floor in a mess onto which tar had been daubed.

Bart hardly glanced at the debris. He hurried toward the back and took a key from his pocket. "They might break that grill, but I'll be damned if I think they could get into my storeroom. And that's where I keep the valuable things like guns and ammunition. I had the doors forged in San Pablo, especially for my purposes. I installed them myself. Ahh!" He turned the key in a heavy lock that pierced the door, and it opened.

Nick examined the door as they passed. Though it was painted brown to match the wood in the store, the door was solid metal—steel perhaps. The paint was scratched badly but the door had stood the test. Bart gave it an affectionate thump as he went by.

The storeroom was untouched, the heavy bars on the windows unscarred. Bart turned on his heel, looking over the orderly stacks of crates, the laden shelves.

"Umm!" he grunted. "Now I'm going over to see Sheriff Tolliver. Look out for things here, will you, Nick?"

Blasingame stared at his cousin. "Bart—" he began, but the younger man shook his head.

"I'm going right now," he said. Then Nick was alone in the mercantile.

CHAPTER EIGHT

This was a Bart that Nick hadn't suspected might exist. Even the set-to of the night before hadn't warned him that the square-built and competent young man whom he had found in Moreno had cut loose his ties from the gentle youth of Baltimore. Except for his pocket pistol, Bart hadn't taken a weapon, Nick realized too late.

The physician chose a hefty twelve-gauge from the stock, broke open a box of shells, and loaded the gun. Then, making certain that his position wasn't visible from the street, he moved to the front of the store and watched as Bart entered the sheriff's office. All his instincts told him to cross the street and go in after him. Then he realized this was Bart's fight. Interference on his part would be unforgivable. Win or lose, Bart was his own man now, and he had to handle this in his own way.

Nevertheless, Nick found cold sweat trickling down his back, though the morning was already thunderously hot. The wooden door across the street was open, but he could see nothing of the interior of the office. No sound of a voice drifted back across the dusty thoroughfare to reach his ears. He needed to twitch and fidget, but he held himself in disciplined steadiness. It seemed to take a geological age for Bart's figure to reappear in the doorway.

Even then, he half-turned and said something to the unseen man inside. Then he started down the two-step descent to the street. Nick tucked the shotgun firmly under his arm and moved to the doorway, keeping his eye on Bart through the remnants of the window. When Bart's boot touched the dust of the street, a lanky man stepped into the open door of the sheriff's office. His hand moved toward his hip.

Nick hot-footed it through the door, shotgun leveled. "I wouldn't do anything foolish," he called to the man across the way. "Accidents do happen, but most of them are caused by fools."

The face that turned toward him was that of the deputy who had tried to kiss Ellen Harper. It was filled with fury, which gave Nick a feeling of warm satisfaction beneath his breastbone. He waved the shotgun barrel gently from side to side.

"Go back in there and be a good boy," he said. "I'll reason with you later." He laughed aloud.

Bart hadn't even looked back when he saw Nick step into the open. As if he were taking a morning stroll, he ambled back to is own place of business and went inside. Nick followed, unloading the shotgun.

Once out of sight, Bart wiped his forehead. "I thought sure he was going to shoot me in the back," he said, sitting down on Alicia's high stool behind the counter. "After what I said to Tolliver, it's a wonder he wasn't the one to follow me out. It wasn't Tolliver, though. I recognized Nat Tully's steps when he came through the door."

"What in the world did you tell that crew?" asked Nick. "I would have given my eyeteeth to follow you across the street and hear you lay them low, but I hated to butt in."

"You don't really want to know," Bart assured him. "To talk to a jackass you have to use jackass language. They know where I stand now. They thought they knew before, but they didn't. Now they do.

"There'll be killing before this is done with, Nick. If it's me, take care of Al and the baby." He rose and set the stool aside.

Nick saw him stoop to begin picking up debris. He went, himself, after Alicia's dustpan and broom. Together, they swept up the broken glass that had protected a display of pocket watches, clasp knives, cufflinks, and studs. All of those seemed to be missing from the mess on the floor, and Nick suspected that the entire law-enforcement staff of Moreno now sported unwonted decorations and timepieces. They looked up at the sound of a cough and saw Doc Pinter peering in the broken door.

"I see you had visitors last night," he observed, picking his way into the store. "I'll send a boy out for Aunt Sary. She'll clean this up for you, while you try to sort out what you can use from the rest of the debris. She'll be glad of the chance to earn two bits."

Bart straightened his cricked back and brushed his forearm across his damp brow. "What would I do without you, Doc? I should have thought of that immediately. And listen...if you see Isaiah Crow, tell him I'd like to see him, will you? I intended to go see him the first thing this morning, but I found this, and I won't have time."

As Doc left, Ellen Harper appeared at the window. Her shocked face glanced through the broken glass and grillwork. Then she was at the door. "My word, Mr. Hazelton, they've done a lot of beastly things, but this is the messiest to date. Could I help you? I've nothing to do until noon. I'd be happy to do what I can."

"If you could possibly sort through the yard goods and ribbons and such—see what can be salvaged. I don't know enough about such stuff to make a good guess. Al would have, but she's not feeling well, this morning."

"She's not ill, is she?" asked the girl, bending to pick up a roll of ribbon that had escaped under a counter. She straightened up and laid the undamaged roll on the splintered countertop.

"Just tired and a bit off her feed," said Nick, before Bart could answer. "We thought she'd do better today just resting. I'm glad we did. This would have upset her greatly. If you'd help us decide on sticky questions—literally sticky, I'm afraid—it would be a big help." he said, glancing at the tarry mess on the floor.

As she moved toward the yard-goods counter, Bart winked at Nick behind her back. Nick felt his face, his reliable poker face, grow warm. Nevertheless, he looked Bart in the eye and raised one eyebrow. "So what?" the gesture said, but his blush contradicted it.

Doc's "Aunt Sary" turned out to be a middle-aged mulatto woman of much presence. She surveyed the wreckage, greeted Bart, Nick, and Ellen, and organized her tactics in one awe-inspiring minute. She put Bart to taking down the damaged grill-work, Ellen to watching the front, re-rolling salvaged ribbons all the while, and then she turned to Nick.

"They say you going to open up nex' to Doc. If'n you don't mind, I 'spects you needs somebody to do for you. That place is in a terrible mess. Mr. Crow kin tell you who to git to do the carpenter work, and when he gets through, jest call me and I'll clean it up for you real good."

Nick found himself walking down the board sidewalk toward the back street before he understood that he had been firmly dismissed and sent about his business. And he had fully intended to spend the day in Ellen's company!

It took only a short time to arrange for workmen to do what he wanted in the office. He got the keys from Hunt and went over to look at the place, where he found a great deal to be done. Partitions had to be built to make a waiting room and an examination room. With so much space to work with, he decided to have two small rooms in the back to use in lieu of old Doctor Harper's "nursing home."

Looking about, he realized that he could create a small bed-sitting room for himself, so that if need be, he could live there as long as any patient remained who needed instant care. Then, too, if he had a difficult confinement coming up, or any case that might require speedy attendance, he could sleep there, saving the long ride out to his prospective home.

Full of plans, he made his way back to the mercantile. He found incredible headway had been made. Already, the damaged counters had been rearranged, their glass removed or mended with cardboard strips. Goods that had escaped the tar brush were neatly arranged on those, and Ellen seemed to be enjoying a brisk trade in materials.

It seemed that everyone who heard about the break-in came into the store and bought something, even if only a paper of pins or a pound of nails. For moral support? Nick suspected as much, and this gave him a rather sneaky notion. Taking up his place near the front door, he made an opportunity to speak with just about every customer before he or she could leave.

"Did you know that Mr. Hazelton has decided to run for mayor? Yes, indeed, I agree that he'd make an excellent one. If you would consider voting for him, we would appreciate it." This varied, of course, in the case of the ladies, who were urged to speak to their husbands about voting for Bart. All in all, the response was positive, though many looked nervously across the street while listening to his sales pitch.

When Bart found out what Nick was doing, he was forced to retire to the store room for some minutes. He emerged with his face still a bit flushed and tears of laughter dampening his eyes.

He found the opportunity to speak to Nick in private, too. "Trust you to use the chance the enemy himself gave us! I swear, Nick, every time I think I'm getting almost grown up and smart, you have to show me how far I still have to go. If we're ever hit by a tornado or torn up by stampeding elephants, I hope you're around. You'll turn it into a profit, while everybody else is sitting around moaning about the mess."

Nick looked blankly at his cousin; then his own lips began to curve upward. With considerable speed, he retired to the storeroom, himself. When he came out again, he said, "Do you believe that I never thought about that angle at all? I just saw all these people going in and out, evidently because they like you and your store. I thought I'd seize the opportunity. It never once dawned on me that if we'd worked a year and hired a brass band, we couldn't have dreamed up a more successful campaign tactic." He choked back a chuckle.

"Here they have direct evidence of the things they know are happening. They know it can happen to them, too. And they understand that the only way to avoid a slam-bang battle and bloodshed is to throw out the present mayor and sheriff. And to think I didn't even see the funny side of it until you showed it to me. Do you suppose I'm getting old, Bart? My sense of humor used to keep me in hot water."

Bart had no chance to reply. He was interrupted by three matrons who showered him with assurances that they would, indeed, urge their husbands to vote for him. He watched them pass the window and turned to Nick.

"Their urgings carry something like the combined weight of all the pyramids of Egypt. If I can get all the middle-aged ladies in town on my side, I'll have the vote. But it's more than likely that won't do us a bit of good.

"They tell me that the election, just before I got here, had a vote count that totaled two and a half times the number of qualified voters in the entire county. That's the reason Tolliver's the sheriff now.

Whitfield pulled off that grand coup, and the people got pretty riled up about it. Even the governor had to say something. But this year only the mayor is up for reelection. Next year will be Tolliver's turn."

"By that time, maybe we will have put spokes in all their wheels," said Nick. Then he frowned. "Can you electioneer by yourself for awhile? I haven't had time to see Robertson about my place. I want to nail it down firmly, before Gussie Moran has time to do her big-blue-eyes bit on him again. I fell in love with that piece of ground as well as the house. I'd like to see how the paperwork is going."

"It should be about ready, as he didn't have to send anything to Mississippi." Bart said. "Be sure to go and see Oren. I think you've earned your keep for the day."

Robertson had he papers prepared and ready to notarize. Nick read through them carefully. Then he glanced up and smiled. "You are meticulous, Mr. Robertson.," he said to the skinny old fellow. "Now if my funds will just come in from Baltimore, we can get this matter finished. I should have word to-morrow. They were going to telegraph the bank here, to hurry things up."

Robertson pushed his glasses onto his forehead and wiped his eyes with a spotless piece of linen. Then he wiped the glasses and resettled them. Nick felt that the old man was preparing to say something that made him uncomfortable. He waited patiently until the lengthy process was completed.

"It has come to my attention," Robertson said at last, "that some people have found the local bank... unreliable. Of course I feel certain that your money will arrive safely. You should have no problem with the transaction. But I feel that you would be well advised to bank in San Pablo." He looked up, squinting.

"It pains me to say this. Moreno has always been my home. My father came here very early... long before the Revolution. Nevertheless, I have heard from those whose words I trust that problems have arisen. *Verbum sapienti*, solely, you understand."

So, Nick thought, even the trusting land-office man is beginning to smell the skunk cabbage in the rose garden. He nodded as Robertson finished.

"I had heard something of the sort; he replied. "My cousins have had some severe trouble with local officials as well. Only this morning, we arrived at the mercantile to find it had been broken into and not only robbed but vandalized. A horrible mess. I find it unthinkable that any civilized town would allow such activities."

Robertson's brow clouded. "Oh, I hate to hear that! I must go over and see if there is anything I can do to help the Hazeltons. They have added much to Moreno since their arrival. They brought with them a great deal of Eastern *savoir faire*. I do hope Mrs. Hazelton was not too much distressed?"

"She remained at home today to rest. We were glad, as it turned out. It would have given her a lot of pain and anger that she doesn't need to cope with. I am sure her husband would be glad to see you, however. Particularly since he intends to make a...political announcement soon. I know he would value your advice in the matter."

Blasingame left the old fellow bustling about, making ready to walk over to the store. Making an excuse, he hurried away, turned the comer, and made a beeline for Bart.

"Robertson would be a good man to have on our side in an election. I'd make book on it. According to him, his family has been here since the Year One...at least before the Anglos took over. He is respected and liked. I've found that in talking with people, and everyone knows he's almost foolishly honest. Ask him sincerely what he thinks of your running for mayor. I think he'll like the idea."

Then the doctor crossed the street again and sat on Doctor Pinter's bench, waiting while the little fellow cut the hair of a portly man in business clothing. Combining dentist with barber in his own person, Doc had also combined the talkativeness of both.

"Glad to see you, Doctor Blasingame. I'd like you to meet Archer Sheley. He is vice president of our bank. A regular customer, I'm happy to say. The doctor is going to make his home here, Mr. Sheley. I'm sure you agree that we needed him very badly."

Butting into the middle of Doc's discourse, Sheley said, "Ah, yes. You have funds arriving, I believe. For purchase of a home indeed. A substantial amount." He showed excellent teeth in a humorless smile.

Nick didn't smile back; the banker's eyes were clearly seeing that money, not Nick's face. "I am buying the Pinkston place from Oren Robertson. As I was transferring funds, I brought down enough to make do until my practice gets well underway."

"I do hope you will deposit the extra sum with us," the man said smoothly. "It is very unsafe to keep large amounts of cash on hand. We solicit new accounts," he said, rising. Doc took the cloth from about Sheley's neck and brushed the loose hair from his coat. "Do think about that, sir. Mr. Andrews, our president, will probably speak with you himself when you pick up the money."

Nick said nothing, though he nodded agreeably as the banker turned to leave. Then he stepped into the chair and leaned back. "Give me a shave, Doc. I find that I pull myself across that scar when I stretch my neck to get at the hard parts."

Pinter whipped up a mug of lather, all the while looking at Nick with a half-grin. "You just set a trap for the entire bank. I'd bet on it. I saw that cat-that-stole-the-cream look in your eye when Sheley was giving his spiel. What in tunket are you planning, Nicholas? And is it worth risking your land money on? That's a careful, slick crew over there."

"Over where? I tried my best to locate the place. Then I gave up and sent the telegram and had Bart send word to the bank to look for the money to come in."

"The storefront two doors up from the mercantile. If you want to meet a bunch of buzzards, go in there some time."

"We shall meet, my friend. Tomorrow the money should arrive. I'll be there as soon as the doors open. All the money I sent for will depart the premises with me. They'll know the amount to the penny. They'll watch it walk out in my pockets, and their mouths will be watering. Then...we'll just see what happens."

"So Carry-Ann told you about her old auntie," Doc mused, slapping on a brush full of lather. "And it gave you ideas. Well, if you can make those bastards eat crow, I'm all for it. Nobody ever deserved it more. If you need my help, just ask. The time seems to have come when we must separate the goats from the sheep here in Moreno. Or it might be more accurate to say we must fence out the wolves from the lambs. They've been living high on mutton for far too long."

Nick grunted very carefully, as the razor glided and scraped about his jaw. His eyes met Doc's, and both pairs were twinkling with wicked mirth.

Chapter Nine

It was with some trepidation that Nick and his cousins approached the mercantile on Monday morning. Another break-in, with attendant damage, would have sent their hearts into their boots, after all the hard work put in cleaning up the mess. Alicia had insisted on coming, too, and Nick was much relieved when they found the place locked tightly and untouched.

There was still much to do—restoring stock to shelves, replacing lost items, repairing counters and cases. Nick left them busy and crossed the street to his own office space. A long, lean man was propped against the front of the building, waiting for him.

"'Lo, Doc. I'm Rafe Ives, come to work on yo' job, here. Mr. Crow done sent me."

Nick nodded as he unlocked the door. "Glad to see you, Rafe. Mr. Crow told me you'd do a good job for me in jig time."

He entered the office and gestured about at the dusty expanse. "I have written out just what I want you to do, with drawings. All you need to do is to follow the instructions."

Ives' sallow face flushed. "Cain't read, Doc. You read it to me. Then I'll know. I kin read plans,

jest cain't read words. And I'll remember everything."

Discomfited, Nick laid the carefully drawn plans
on the table that he had scrounged from Isaiah Crow
and bent over them. Doubting the usefulness of this,
he read slowly through the instructions.

When he had finished, Rafe fixed his gaze
mournfully on the wall above the physician's head
and recited, word for word, the entire lengthy
document. Blasingame was surprised at the flypaper
accuracy of the man's verbal memory. Impressed,
he went over the drawings, pacing out on the dusty
floor the dimensions of the different spaces to be
partitioned.

He found that the man had many useful sugges-
tions. The positioning of doors, allocations of space,
openings for ventilation seemed to be instinctive
with him.

The time went quickly. Nick realized at last that
it must be nearing the time when the bank would
open. His money should be there, and he intended to
be on the spot at once.

Leaving his project in capable hands, he crossed
the street again, angling toward the signless storefront Doc had pointed out to him. He glanced
through the plate-glass window as he passed it. Beyond, he could see Sheley talking with someone
who was out of sight behind a shoulder-high parti-
tion.

A raucous bell jangled as he pushed through the
door. Sheley's head came around. Then the man
smiled broadly at Blasingame and held out his hand.
"Happy to see you, Doctor. We received your funds
this morning. Right on schedule. Come and meet

110

my associates. They're anxious to make your acquaintance."

Nick kept a poker face as he was introduced to Calvin Andrews and Job Wylie. It wasn't easy, for Andrews was the very image of a redneck hayseed. His expensive suit and carefully shined shoes seemed incongruous on his scroungy body. The long-skulled, pale-eyed face was out of place above the opulence below it. Only the shrewd flicker of the eyes told Nick that this man was far more sophisticated and knowledgeable than his appearance indicated.

Wylie was different. He was short, thick-bodied, and still youngish, in a bull-faced way. Nick suspected that he might well have been the teller who sent the deputy after Carry-Ann's auntie for the second time. The way he was handling the money he counted into the teller's drawer said a lot about his reverence for the stuff. He all but caressed the thick bundles of greenbacks as he laid them into the spaces.

The amenities over, Nick said, "I would like to pick up the cash now, gentlemen. I want to finish up my business in short order. I feel that as time goes on, my opportunities to work on my place and my office may become few and far between. I'll probably be very busy once people learn that I'm here. Do you mind if we get on with it?"

"Not at all," Andrews said. He went to his desk and opened a drawer. "We would very much like you to deposit the full amount with us. You can easily write checks for any operating funds you might need. I know that Oren would be glad to take your check."

Nick sighed, hoping he wasn't overdoing his act. "I really am sorry, Mr. Andrews. I feel sure that your institution is a fine one, but I had a terrible experience with one of the banks back in Maryland. It has shaken my confidence in them. I hope to do everything strictly with cash for now. Perhaps in time I'll come to feel more secure, but at this time I'm really nervous when my money is in the hands of a financial institution."

"Too bad," said Sheley, coming from the direction of the vault with a packet. As he approached, Andrews put back into his drawer the sheaf of papers he had withdrawn.

"We can understand your position. Too many banks are carelessly run," Sheley said. "Here, Calvin, count this out. I already did, but we want it done in the doctor's presence, too."

The count was made. The papers of receipt were signed. Nick left the bank with thirteen thousand dollars in his pocket. He made a beeline to Robertson's office, where he paid over five thousand at once in full payment for his property. With efficiency, the deal was complete, and he left with the deed to his own farm and home in his wallet. Free and clear of all impediments, the instrument stated. It felt wonderful.

But it made him nervous to have so much cash still in his possession. Remembering Bart's ironclad storeroom, he hurried over to the mercantile. Bart was in the storeroom, taking out stock to replace things missing from his shelves.

"Do you suppose you can hide eight thousand dollars so that nobody would suspect it's here?" he asked.

Bart swallowed hard. "If they didn't get in the last time, I doubt they'll be able to unless they try dynamite. And that isn't totally impossible. Our safe is a good one, but any safe can be opened, and that is where they'd look. Hmmm...I know—here!"

He dumped most of the contents of a keg of nails onto a tarp. "We bury your money deep in the nail keg, wrapped in that strip of leather on the shelf over there. That's right: tie it up tight, so it won't unroll. Doesn't make too big a wad, does it? Now scrunch it up a few times. Make it look like a scrap of leather. Now!"

They interred the wad of leather and cash in the keg. They were careful to pick up every stray nail and replace it in the keg. Then they looked at each other with satisfaction.

"Who says you're not getting smart in your old age?" asked Nick. "And who, in his right mind, is going to look into a keg of nails for money when there's a big, strong safe right under his nose?" You're bright, my son. Very bright."

Bart grinned. "I'll be worried, too, until whoever you're conning or whatever you're cooking up comes to a head. The thought of all that money lying around in there gives me the shivers."

They said nothing to Alicia, who was engaged in helping a young woman choose dress material. Nick nodded to an incoming customer and left the store. His own office needed his attention, but he detoured by way of Doc Pinter's bailiwick.

At the moment there was no customer there, and that suited his purposes. "If anybody should ask, Doc, could you tell them that I went into the bakery, into the bank, over to Crow's, and just about everywhere else this morning? They may not ask, but just in case they should?"

Doc's eyes twinkled. "Oh, I'll help you set a trap, Nick. Don't worry about that. I take it that you've hidden your excess funds in a safe place and don't want anyone to be able to deduce where they are. At least, not too easily."

"You're a smart old bird, do you know that?" asked Nick. "I just hope that none of the opposition are as wily as you are. I'll be up the creek—and out a lot of cash—if they are."

"Have no fear. They are crooked, mean, lawless, callous, cruel, shrewd in an irrational sort of way, but few are intelligent. Not even Tom Moran, who has built a fortune with his own hands. Some men have a talent for making money that has nothing whatever to do with brains."

"What about Augusta? She struck me as being a bright woman!'

"If Augusta had not been born beautiful, she would have been frighteningly brilliant. Fortunately for the world, her looks were such that she has never had to use the mind ticking away beneath that glorious hair. It's rusted into tight channels. Possibly she couldn't use it now to full advantage. Thinking well requires constant practice, you know." He sighed. "The manipulation of men, if you look like Gussie Moran, requires no conscious thought at all."

Nick laughed. He well knew that to be true. He had seen friends and colleagues reduced to apparent idiocy by young women who looked like angels and had all the intellectual capacity of angel-food cake. Thank God for small favors! Alicia had spoiled him for the company of stupid women.

"Thank you, Doc. I'll go and see how Rafe is coming along with the work next door. Come by when you get the chance, and I'll show you how we're going to fix it up."

"Now there's someone who was born with nothing except brains," Doc commented. "Rafe is homely as a mud fence. He was born to the poorest of the poor and never had a chance to educate himself. But he has a first-class mind. He can deliver a message verbatim. He can remember what you said to him ten years ago last Tuesday in minute detail. He can look at any problem of a practical nature and solve it in one breath. If he had had Gussie's chances...oh, well. Futility, thy name is speculation. Go along and see to your new space. I'll be along later."

Nick found that Rafe had already arranged the lumber, hardware, and nails that Bart had provided in neat and ready-for-action stacks and piles. The studding for a good quarter of the partitions was up, and the place was taking shape as if by magic.

"I'll have to admit, Rafe, that Mr. Crow understated your abilities," he said, as the lean man looked up to greet him. "You are faster than fast. I have an idea. Maybe you might want to think about it, while you do this job."

Rafe measured another stud while Nick continued, "I'm going to want my house finished. I've just bought the Pinkston place, out east of town. There's going to be a lot of work to do, building outbuildings and barns and such. I'd like to contract for your work. Maybe for the next year or so. You could do outside work, when it came along, but you'd always have my stuff to keep you busy in between.

"It would give you a steady income that you could depend on. You might even live out there while you're on the job. There's plenty of room, and it would save a lot of time." He had another thought.

"Maybe, in the long haul, you might like to become a sort of overseer for me. I won't have time to tend to any livestock I may accumulate. I don't like to have servants. That sets my teeth on edge. If I could have a man with good sense who would take care of things for me, it would make my life a lot easier. Do you have a family?"

Ives was looking at him a bit blankly, as if too much information had hit him at one time. He seemed to be having trouble assimilating it. But he cleared his throat and spat.

"Got a wife and three chillun," he said. "Have kind of a hard time taking care of 'em, too. Ain't all that many jobs around, and I got no land. I'll think on it. Sounds to be a good deal, can we work it out."

Seeing that Rafe worked better when alone, Nick made a few complimentary comments about the neatness of his work. Then he left to stand on the sidewalk, a bit disconsolate.

At last he went to the livery stable, hitched up his buggy, and sped away to the mine. A call on his two patients wouldn't come amiss, he was sure. He also wanted another look at the mine operation itself. He had been too busy with Old Ham to observe the machinery Doc found to be so lacking. It was possible that Hermann Wald might let him look around, very quietly.

It was past noon. The sun was already blazing down, and moist heat rose from the earth and the forest. The dust that was kicked backward by

Lance's hooves stuck uncomfortably on Nick's sweaty face. He shrugged out of his black coat with some difficulty. The crease in his shoulder was still stiff. When the breeze stirred across his damp white shirt, he sighed gratefully.

The road was crooked, following the contours of the land, the winding of a creek, and the corners of properties that had been surveyed but not yet fenced. Nick was moving slowly so as not to heat Lance too much. He came round a right-angle bend very quietly.

Another rig was drawn up beneath a huge magnolia that leaned over the roadway beside a track leading away into thick forest on the right. He was certain that it was the same carriage Augusta Moran had driven when he last saw her. He pulled up beside it.

There was no sign of an occupant. The reins were tied loosely, so the horses could crop the lush grass beside the road, and that indicated to Nick that someone had gone into the wood. That was no concern of his, but something nagged at him as he pulled away toward the mine.

Augusta Moran's parasol lay on the seat of the abandoned rig. He felt he should have deduced something from that, but he couldn't come up with anything significant. Still, the thought that he had last seen St. John riding in that carriage kept creeping into his mind.

He found Old Ham sitting on his front porch. Nick walked around him, shaking his head. Then he turned to the old woman who sat in a rocking chair, spitting snuff delicately into a can.

"I wish you were a little younger, Old Ma'am. If

I had a nurse like you to call on, I'd set up a real hospital, and we'd both get rich. I never saw anything like it. What did you do? I didn't expect him to be this far along for weeks."

"Give him yarb tea, Doctuh. Put aloes on the bad places, too. That stuff the bes' for healin' that you ever did see. Done traded for a bunch of it with the Mex'kins. I raises it inside the house in buckets. You like to see 'em?"

Intrigued, Nick followed her into the dim depths of the little shack. The back room was a kitchen, and there he found a row of pots sitting on a shelf below an open shutter that was the only window in the room. He looked at the notch-edged plants with some interest. The wounds had healed cleanly, without a trace of infection. If there existed a plant that could induce such healing, he was curious about it, whether or not his medical school *confrères* might approve.

"You likes to have one, you's welcome to it," said Old Ma'am. "Here's de biggest one. I calls it Rosie. Names all my plants. You kin take it, iffen you wants it."

Nick took the pot carefully in both hands. "Thank you, Old Ma'am. I'm interested in this. I'll try it on other patients, along with the other medications I have, and we'll see which does the best job. Now I'd better go see to Lucy Wald."

"She doing fine," the old woman volunteered. "And that baby—he's the wisest young'un I ever did see. They be glad to see you."

They were. Lucy was sitting up in bed. The house was neat, and her bedding was clean. Hermann and her neighbor were living up to their commitments.

Mother and child were flourishing. He stood to leave at last, looking down at his patient. "You might try getting up a bit, Lucy. Say next week. Go easy, and be sure that Hermann is here to help you. You're going to be weak as water for a while. Just be careful and use common sense. You've just about got this thing under control now."

"Thank you, Doctor. You be good to me. Everyone have been good. Even Mrs. Moran, she come out to see me this morning. That Mr. St. John, he go to the mine, and she take the time to visit me. America is fine place, *nicht wahr?*"

Nick agreed, but a warning signal went up in his mind. He took the road back to Moreno at a good clip, ignoring the heat. He kept his eyes peeled for the rig he had seen earlier. Though he had been at least two hours at the mine, the rig was still there. The team had tired of grazing and were standing with their eyes half-closed, one hind hoof cocked at that impossible angle achieved only by a bored horse. There was no sound from the wood. Nick pulled up, spoke to Lance, and jumped down.

He carefully examined the track that led into the wood. There were two sets of footprints, one small and high-heeled. More importantly, he found a stake driven into the deep mulch beneath the magnolia that shaded the carriage. Another was deeper into the forest. Fetching about, he found yet another in a straight line with the first two. Someone had surveyed the tract recently, for the stakes hadn't weathered a bit.

He climbed back into the buggy very thoughtfully. It might be that this was Moran land. The

PRESCRIPTION FOR DANGER, BY ARDATH MAYHAR

mine was only a couple of miles farther up the road. Perhaps Gussie was showing it to St. John., He might even be buying the property.

But something in his instinct said no. That was too straightforward for people like the Morans. Not to mention St. John. He had a feeling, deep in his gut, that the land belonged to someone else. Perhaps to a newcomer, or to someone who lived elsewhere. Someone who might be hornswoggled out of the land.

That hunch was so strong that he hurried to Oren Robertson's office once he reached town. It was late, almost closing time. Robertson, however, was a widower and welcomed any excuse to delay his lonely homecoming. He obligingly took down his big map, detailed enough, though some spaces were simply marked "forest."

Nick traced the road he had traveled, counting bends and right angles. "Here!"

He leaned forward. "This is the third-to-last right-angle bend before you get to the mine. There's the grandfather of all magnolia trees leaning over a track that goes back into the woods at an angle. I'd like to know if it's part of a grant. Who does it belong to? Would it be any trouble to find out?"

Robertson chuckled dryly. "No trouble at all. I won't even have to look it up. I sold it six months ago to a party in Louisiana. He intended to move his family here at once, but his wife became ill, and he had to delay. Gabriel Mouton—that's the name. Thibodeaux is his hometown. Should be coming out before too long.

"That's a beautiful tract of forest, part of the original Moreno holding. If it hadn't been sold already, I'd have asked you to look at it before you bought. There's a meadow that borders on the river—it could be the original 'green pastures' they talk about in the psalm."

"Thank you, sir," said Nick, straightening up. "I was just curious. I hoped you'd be patient enough to tell me what I wanted to know, and I'm happy it was so easy. You must have almost every piece of land around here right at your fingertips."

"I've been at it for thirty years," Robertson answered, rolling the map and setting it back on the shelf amid a cloud of dust. "You should have seen my office before I built this one. Pine planks, warped by the sun. No room to speak of. I'm so proud of my new building, I nearly bust my buttons every time I unlock the door. Really, anyone who has seen every land transaction here go on before his eyes for that length of time can't help but recall what belongs to whom."

With another word of thanks, Nick left the office. He looked up the street, and he found that the sun was now just above the tops of the trees on the west. It was almost time to close the mercantile.

He shivered a little, though the day was steaming with heat reflected from the streets, as well as broiling in the direct rays of the sun.

Tonight, he mused, might well see the springing of his trap. Excitement thrilled lightly along his nerves. He hadn't felt like this since his first day in the dissecting rooms in the days of his training.

He ambled toward the store. There he found Bart about to lock up, which he did with even more than his usual care, and he followed the Hazelton rig toward home. He must, he knew, behave absolutely normally, or Alicia would sniff out his plan.

She had an uncanny knack of reading him. He had to avoid that, for he didn't want either of his cousins to be involved in any way with what he intended to do that night.

He had set the trap. He was the one who had to deal with the result if it were sprung by his quarry.

CHAPTER TEN

It was a long evening. Bart and Alicia insisted on taking coffee out onto the veranda after the meal. They sat through the short twilight, watching the fireflies flicker across the lawn. It seemed to be a time for reminiscences, and in spite of the difficulty of concealing his impatience, Nick found himself enjoying the intimate "do-you-remembers" that the three of them shared.

Darkness fell. The moon, almost full, rose in the east, and mosquitoes began to hum about their ears. They regretfully broke up their conclave and went into the house, which sported wire screening. This was an almost unheard-of luxury and had been brought at great expense from the East when Bart first understood the miserable nature of summers in East Texas. All the stinging, swarming insects that bred in the fields and swamps were merciless.

Alicia proposed continuing the conversation in the living room. Nick, however, pleaded fatigue caused by his sore shoulder, a convenient excuse, and went to his room. He listened for a long time as his cousins stirred about the house. At last their door closed, and he heaved a sigh of relief. He had no intention of endangering Bart with his plot or of leaving Alicia alone in the house, while the two of them reconnoitered his trap. It was much simpler to carry out the plan on his own.

He gave them time to settle into sleep. Then he carefully unfastened his screened window and dropped into the cape jasmine bush below.

The deep greenery, scented with a few late blossoms, swished quietly about him as he paused to listen again. Then he headed for the stable. He made a habit of leaving Lance in a stall with a good ration of oats, for a doctor never knew when a midnight call might come. Now he saddled the gelding in the dark and led him up the drive to the road. He kept a hand over his nostrils, so he couldn't whicker.

Lance wasn't used to being ridden, though he had been broken to the saddle, so Nick proceeded sideways down the road for several rods until he convinced the horse that he knew what he was doing and meant what he said. Then they stepped out easily, following the moon-silvered dust of the track.

It wasn't more than two or three miles to town. The moon was still below the zenith when Nick drew rein and hitched Lance behind Isaiah Crow's shop on the back street.

There were two ways of getting onto Main Street from there. He could follow the cross street to the corner opposite the sheriff's office, or he could go the long way around the block, then eastward past the bank. Nick decided against the short way. He couldn't be sure who was holding the fort at the sheriff's office. Someone might still be there, and he didn't want to alert anyone of his return to town to reach the enemy.

Earlier, he had poked around, looking for a better approach to the mercantile, and had found one. At the back of Mrs. Flanders' bakery, there was a latticework, up which she had trained morning glories. It ended just below the window at the end of the hall serving the offices on the second floor. He went up the lattice more easily than he had expected, his wound having healed enough to be flexible and only minimally sore.

The window wasn't locked. He hadn't expected it to be, for there was nothing in the hall and each office was locked individually. Blessing the fact that the window was opened during the day to let in a breeze, he went through it quietly and perched on the sill. Because the hall was uncarpeted, he removed his boots before setting foot on the bare boards.

At the top of the steep stairway leading down to the street, he paused for a long moment, listening. There was no sound from below. He moved quietly down until he could see across to the sheriff's office, next to the darkened saloon. A dim light glimmered in the window, and he guessed that someone was in the rear office, which overlooked the three cells.

The street was lit by the nearly full moon. That made the black tunnels under the store awnings even better concealment. Nick stepped out, still unbooted, and made his way to the mercantile. The door was firmly locked. No light showed from inside, and no sound broke the stillness. Knowing the imperviousness of the rear walls, Nick decided that his best move would be to wait across the street in his own office. From there, he could see if anyone approached the mercantile from the front. He would be hidden until action might be called for.

He ducked across the still street and into his unlocked office in one swift motion. Rafe had convinced him it was best to leave it unlocked, as it would save replacing the excellent door.

"If the sheriff takes a notion to git some of your lumber or nails, he's going to do hit. If he's got to bust down the door, then he'll do that, too. Locks ain't kept him outen many places. Look at Mr. Hazelton's store. You got to line a place with iron, if'n you intend to keep Tolliver outen hit. I helped Mr. Hazelton fix up his back room. That's the oliest way to do hit."

Nick grinned into the darkness. He took the small table he had borrowed from Crow and set it gently before the big window. Just beyond the hem of moonlight, he perched on the edge, watching the street for any activity.

The night wore away. The moon crossed over to the west a bit, slanting its rays more deeply. Nick decided that his bait was not going to be taken and that his night's vigil had been a waste of time. He had risen, stretching his cramped muscles, when a sudden scuffle of sound brought him to attention.

He moved nearer to the corner of the window and looked cautiously into the street. There was nobody to be seen. The window of the mercantile reflected a wash of light from the moonlit dust of the street, and there was no interruption of its glare.

The sound came again. Nick realized that it was on his side of the street—boots moving on the boardwalk. He cat-footed across the office and laid his ear against his door. He heard the door into the sheriff's office open; the sound carried through the wall plainly. Someone had come up the boardwalk from the east and entered the place very quietly.

Did this have something to do with his trap? Nick whirled to the window and watched again. Fifteen minutes crept by according to the moonlit face of his watch. Nothing stirred. Fifteen more. Still nothing.

So. Maybe this had nothing to do with his eight thousand dollars after all. Perhaps there was some sort of secret meeting going on right now in Tolliver's office.

Nick glanced at his high ceiling, dim in the tenuous light. Above it, he knew, was space for additional offices, should the need arise. They hadn't been finished, and no stair had been built to give access. Rafe, however, had shown him a scuttle hole in his own ceiling that led into that extra area. Rafe's ladder stood against the wall.

In a few seconds, Nick was straining at the hatch-like cover leading into the upper part of the building. It gave reluctantly, but it went quietly. He heaved himself up into pitch darkness.

The place was sickeningly hot and stuffy, smelling of pine resin, dust, rat runs, and something indefinable. But now he could hear voices quite clearly. He looked down at the hole into his office, plainly visible because of the feeble backwash of light from the moon. Nick wriggled cautiously toward the source of the sounds he heard, stopping directly above them.

"...Couldn't've known ahead of time!" protested a voice. "It happened too quick. Nobody knowed Miz Hazelton had any cousin, much less that he was coming to live here! This deal's been cooking for eight months now. Who'd've thought a man who's just got here would jump in so quick and buy a place? It's just bad luck, all around. I think we'd better cut our losses and get out of it. Write him that we've found a flaw in the title or something."

"And send back all that money?" This was a voice Nick had heard before. Archer Sheley had a prim manner of speaking that identified itself instantly. "That's a lot to lose. Is there no way we can retrieve our position?"

"Maybe. It's risky, though. Our man is no fool. Except, of course, for wanting to buy land he's never seen. He can read deeds as if they were primers. He paces distances and finds markers. It's just barely possible that we can palm off the place Gussie has shown to St. John this afternoon, if we set false markers. It's a risky business, Arch. It might be safer to take what we've got and clean out of the game."

There came a pause. Nick used the opportunity to set things straight in his mind Obviously, Sheley and someone (he felt certain the unknown voice must belong to Tom Moran) had sold the Pinkston place to a third party. But five thousand dollars seemed a paltry sum to merit such an elaborate set-up—unless the Pinkston tract was only a part of the land thus sold. Perhaps giving access to the road—or the river! Hmmm. And the place Augusta had shown this afternoon was also a big tract, Robertson had said. Giving access to the river—and part of it was sold, evidently without Moran and his henchmen knowing about it.

So Doc Pinter had been correct. It was a land swindle that had brought St. John to Moreno. Evidently the petty thieveries in town and around the countryside were only the perquisites of the flunkies. The big money lay in land, as it usually did.

Sheley was speaking again. "Think about the advance money we'll have to dig up! The shares alone will cost us a bundle. Why didn't St. John warn us that this was a dangerous prospect who might come down to look over his investments? We should have been told. It's inexcusable!"

"It was worse than careless. I'm not at all certain that St. John is being entirely square with us. I get the feeling, lately, that he's playing his own game. He was completely convincing up there in Memphis, but now I begin to wonder. He has handled a lot of money for us. Are we completely sure we've received all we are supposed to?" The second voice died into a pregnant silence. Nick stifled a sneeze with one hand and knelt on the dusty floor in order to hear even better.

"We can handle it, I calculate." This was the first time Nick had heard this voice. He tried to recall if it might be Tolliver's. The few times he'd talked with Tolliver, the man's vocal characteristics had made no impression on him.

"If you can get the tract out toward the mine all staked and faked, it will work. That Eastern dude won't stay any longer than he has to. They never do. If the heat don't get 'em, the bugs do. He'll hightail it back to Ohio as soon as he's convinced the land's there and properly marked. We'll just have to make for damn sure he don't talk to Robertson. That old idiot could shoot the entire deal to hell and gone."

There was no sound. Nick could imagine a concerted sigh of frustration going the rounds of the conspirators below him. Then Sheley's voice again: "About Robertson. It's his fault we're in this bind. If he'd thrown in with us, when we sounded him out, there'd have been no problem. We could've cut him in for a share, sold the same tracts time and time again, and nobody would have ever been the wiser. It wouldn't make a damn if we didn't have any right to sell the property, if he'd wake up and see where the profit lies."

"Arch, I keep telling you that Oren is another breed of cat. I 'sounded him out,' as you call it, so carefully you wouldn't believe it. Didn't more than hint in the most hypothetical way that somebody might find it profitable to falsify sales of properties. He nearly messed his pants. It took all Gussie's big-eyed blarney to convince him that we were just concerned because we'd heard of something like that being done someplace else.

"Lord, I thought he was going to take the next train to see the governor. He thinks deeds and abstracts and Spanish grants are Holy Writ; meddling with them would be blasphemy to him.

"No, there's no way we can square Robertson. We'll have to get him out of town when Blunt comes. Something long and involved that he has to take to the state capital."

"Maybe...permanently?" purred Sheley. "Lots of things can happen to a man who goes traveling around the country. Accidents. Stray bullets. Train robberies. Even things like mistaken identities in feuds. There are a lot of possibilities. Tollie, here, knows. It would untie our hands if we could get one of our own people into the land office."

"I don't want to know anything about it," said

Moran, his tone brusque. "Do what you want to, both of you. I like to make money as well as anybody, but I won't conspire to do murder. Unless, of course, it's that damn nephew of Gussie's. I wish that doctor had done a final job on him, while he was after him."

"It's a shame Hobie didn't do a better job on the doctor," came the reply. "That would've saved a lot of trouble all along the line. One of us could've offered to buy out his place from his cousin. That would've put us all in the clear for the whole three thousand acres. It's really a pity."

"What?" asked Tolliver.

"That Gussie didn't teach that kid to shoot as well as to lie and to steal."

"That is quite enough," said Moran. "You won't talk about my wife in front of me, whatever you say behind our backs. She has her faults, has Gussie, but think—how could we have gotten where we are without her? She figures out half our plans. She hornswoggles suspicious bankers and land men and the general public. She's our ace in the hole, gentlemen, and don't you forget it. Without her, Robertson would have caught us out ten times over."

"You're right," grunted Tolliver. "So why don't we see what she can do with that ornery Eastern doctor? He's been nothing but trouble since he got here. I can't prove it, but I'd bet my eyeteeth he and his cousins were the ones that broke up the cattle drive, the other night. Gussie's never had a failure yet. Sic her onto him. She might be able to keep him busy enough so he'll keep his nose out of our business until we can see to Blunt."

There was a rumble of ribald laughter. Nick smiled wickedly into the blackness. That could be an interesting encounter. Or series of encounters. If he led her up the garden path for long enough, he just might be able to throw a few spokes into several wheels.

There was a scuffling of feet. Chairs were shoved back protestingly over pine floors. Evidently the meeting was about to break up. Nick backed cautiously toward the gap of dim light, afraid to turn in case he might stumble over something he couldn't see. That did him no good at all. His heel hit something solid, and he sat loudly and suddenly on a floor that clattered with loose scraps of lumber.

He remained still as death, as those below him regained their wits and began to mutter. When they fell silent, he knew they were listening for any more movement above them. Only when they moved toward the door to the street did he rise and make for the scuttle hole.

He had left the office door unlocked as he had found it. They'd be inside in a shake. Backing into the hatch, he grabbed the handholds and let his legs dangle until they found the ladder. Hooking his toes under a rung, he hauled first himself and then the ladder painfully through the hatch into the loft. Then, as he heard fumbling at the front door, he drew the hatch cover over the hole, leaving a crack in order to see who came into the office.

They came in carefully as if expecting an ambush. The moonlight was pretty far down, but there was still enough to light the room dimly. Tolliver had also brought a lantern, and they had it alight in a moment. Nick could see its wavering light dance about, making the shadows undulate.

They examined every cranny of the place, tried the back door, which had been nailed shut at some time in the past and hadn't yet been unfastened. Sheley glanced up, searching the ceiling, and Tolliver obligingly held up the lantern so they could inspect the opening they knew was there.

Nick hoped devoutly that he had left no dirty fingerprints visible on the underside of the hatch. That would be a dead giveaway. But Sheley grunted, and the lantern swung down again.

"Could have been a rat," observed Tolliver.

"Goddamned *big* rat," said Moran, whom Nick recognized as the heavyset man he had seen from a distance a few days before.

"There might well have been something in here that fell, and we only thought it was above us," said Sheley. He turned his attention to the piles of lumber and kegs of nails and hardware.

"That stack there. See how it's tumbled around? Rafe Ives is doing the work here. He's neater than any man has a right to be. He never would have left it that way. Probably a cat or something, maybe even that big rat you mentioned, went scurrying across it and knocked something loose so the whole thing went."

Nick blessed his awkwardness in moving the table to the window. He had disarranged Rafe's careful pile himself.

"Could be." Moran's tone was still doubtful. "If anybody was here he's gone now. Couldn't've been upstairs, without a way to climb. These ceilings are fourteen feet, if they're an inch. I guess you're right, Arch. We'd better get out of here. Wouldn't want to leave any sign we've been here. It would bring that doctor sniffing around our heels, for sure. He might think we didn't see through that scheme about his cash. Thinks we're fools."

They tramped out. Nick could hear their heels on the boardwalk, as they made their way back next door. He suspected that they, too, had concealed their horses someplace.

Once they were gone, he let the ladder down carefully, so as not to disturb the deputy he knew was on duty next door. It was a relief to get out of the stuffy heat of the loft. He perched again on his table to get his breath and his bearings.

If his trap had been a failure, it had still served him well. If he hadn't caught someone red-handed in the act of breaking into the mercantile, he had learned many things he could never have known with any certainty. He had been handed a plateful, indeed.

Possible murder, for one thing. He knew he had to find a way to safeguard Oren Robertson, though it would seem odd if he suddenly appointed himself the man's constant companion.

Falsification of deeds, trusts, line markers, and God knew what else. Plain and ordinary swindling, though of a high-class caliber. He knew so much now that it was an embarrassment. Knowing without any proof wasn't much good. Even with proof, it wasn't much better, as he had found to his cost in Baltimore.

He knew one thing. He had to take Alicia and Bart into his confidence. They needed to know what was going on in Moreno, particularly since their store had been vandalized.

Nick rode home slowly. The night had been well spent, but he knew he wouldn't sleep. There was too much to think about.

CHAPTER ELEVEN

He waited until all three had arrived in Moreno the next morning to broach the subject of his midnight adventure. While Rafe measured and sawed and hammered in his office, he took refuge with his cousins, interrupted only by a medical emergency in the guise of a big splinter in young Isaiah Crow's toe.

When Nick finished telling his tale, Bart nodded briefly, but his brow was wrinkled with thought. "That makes a lot of sense," the younger man said at last. "It fits in with everything else. Where all the big fish are wrong'uns, the little fish are going to follow suit. Just one thing really bothers me—how in hell are we going to persuade Oren Robertson that Angel-Face Moran's intimates intend to kill him?"

Nick sighed. "I've been wondering about that. I know you've been friendly with him. How friendly? Socially? Enough to invite him out for a visit? No, that won't work. We're in town most of the time. You can't leave a guest at your home by himself. It's really a problem." Nick rubbed his chin and stared hopefully at Alicia.

She quirked her mouth as if she understood that

he'd been expecting her to come up with a solution at once. "Why not give him something real to do?" she asked. "You have a lot of property in Baltimore that your mother left. It's never been divided, and there's only you and your brother to share it. Neither one of you has bothered to do the job, and now you're way down here, out of pocket, in case he needs to sell something or rent something. You need a good land man. An honest one, who knows values and can size up the fiscal situation."

Nick was beginning to smile.

"Someone like Oren," she went on. "He could go to Maryland as your agent. There isn't all that much to do here, and what there is at this time of year can be handled by his clerk. It will take him several weeks, and by then this man Blunt may have come and gone. And with him the need to get rid of poor old Oren."

Her cousin was grinning widely, now, and her husband was looking smug. "I've never put an impossible situation before her, even in jest, that she didn't come up with a solid gold, foolproof, fourteen-carat solution," Nick said to Bart.

Bart patted his wife's shoulder. "Why do you think I keep her around? She's not much good for anything else, you must admit, but as a planner, she's topnotch."

She bared her teeth, made a swipe at him with the feather duster with which she had been dusting the racks of thread spools. Bart laughed and backed away.

"So now all we have to do is propose the scheme to him," said Nick. "And now that we've settled that, what do you think about this land swindle? Is there anything we can do there to put a spoke into their wheels? I'd like to see this man Blunt alone to fill him in on the scheme, but that isn't going to be easy. They'll watch him like a hawk and guard him as if he were a gold shipment while he is in Moreno. I wonder...will they go to meet him someplace? Or send St. John to do that?"

"Send St. John," said Bart. "He made the original deal, it seems from what you overheard. They'll send him to meet Blunt at Shreveport, most likely, if they don't send him all the way to Ohio. They don't want just anybody talking to him, you can be sure of that. A hell of a lot of conversation takes place on trains, and they can't know who may be traveling along with their pigeon."

Nick nodded. "We'll just have to bide our time and watch for a chance. I wish we knew what else they were cooking up. They talked as if this isn't the first time they've pulled this sort of stunt. And," he said with a smug look, "the plan to sic Augusta on me. I'm looking forward to that!"

Alicia brandished her feather duster. "I'll just wager that you are! You claim to be immune, but you haven't seen strong men turn into jelly at a glance from those eyes as I have. She's one of those women, and don't you doubt it. The sort Gramma warned you against. Oh, yes, I was hiding in the china closet, listening, when she had her talk with you.

"You were about sixteen, and I couldn't have been more than eight or nine. It made me angry when Gramma sent me out of the room to talk to you. I went around to the dining room and listened through the thin spot in the wall where the old door used to be."

Bart burst into laughter. "You always were a little devil!" He turned to Nick. "She decided long ago that she owns at least a half-interest in you. If you think you have any private business, you'd do just as well to figure Allie in on it as a silent partner from the beginning. She's going to be right in the middle of it, like it or not."

"That's fine with me," Nick answered. "Having seen Augusta Moran, I like to think that there's some oasis of good sense and straight talk that I can run to if I find myself outgunned."

"Good," said Alicia. "Now hear this straight talk. Go right now and ask Oren if he'll go to Baltimore for you. We don't know when they expect Blunt. We don't know how soon they'll try to send Oren off on some wild goose chase. Get to him now, set it up, and get him into the clear. Then we can sit down and plot with clear consciences. If plotters ever *have* clear consciences," she added.

"Now there speaks Miss Atherton at her pious worst," said Nick. "I'll go, fellow conspirators, and do my duty. Then we'll put our heads together and conspire!" He bared his teeth in a fiendish grimace, and she fled, laughing, toward her desk.

He found Oren Robertson sitting pensively at his own desk, watching the scanty traffic on his back street. He glanced up, pleased, when Nick entered the office.

"I was hoping you would stop by from time to time," the old man said. "There aren't many new people coming to Moreno yet, and all too many of my old friends have gone to their rewards. What can I do for you today?"

"You can do me a favor," said Nick. "It may, indeed, be too much to ask of such a new acquaintance, and I find myself hesitant to broach the subject."

Robertson's expression brightened with interest. He leaned across his desk to push a pile of dusty books from the visitor's chair. "Sit down and tell me about it. I find myself singularly idle this spring. Something to fill my hours would be most welcome."

Nick sat in the stained leather chair and leaned back. He found it easy to talk to the old fellow, and soon the tale of his maternal inheritance was told. "So there it has lain, undivided and almost untended with more than casual interest, for almost six years. My brother trusts me. I trust him. But now that I'm down here, days away by train, if he should suddenly need to make a major decision, he would be in a pickle."

He frowned. "I hate sending personal or confidential family business over the wires. I need someone to go to Baltimore for me—someone who knows about titles and transfers and powers of attorney and such matters. You can trust my brother implicitly. Anything he wants done, feel free to do on my behalf. Dividing land, selling property—he will know best about all of that. I will, if you accept, give you a limited power of attorney to act for me."

Robertson looked wistful. "It would be a most interesting thing to do," said Robertson, his expression wistful. "And I believe that I could do a bang-up job for you. But why don't you return and do it all yourself?"

Nick settled back more comfortably in the chair.

"I left Baltimore in great anger and hurt. I was all but driven out of my native city because I tried to right some very terrible wrongs. At this moment, I never want to see the city again. In years to come, when I have had time to overcome my feelings, to cool off so to speak, I may return there. But for now, I hate the thought of going back. I have a new life here, new work, and new friends. When you have been mistreated as I have been by old and trusted friends, you truly want to shake the dust of the place off your feet and never go back again."

"I've never been farther than Memphis," Robertson said. "I have some acquaintances in Maryland, however. And New York and Pennsylvania—all over that area, in fact. I have done business with many Eastern concerns, and in the process I have made some good friends, whom I have never met except through correspondence. And never expected to meet, I might add."

"Then this is the time to meet them!" Nick exclaimed. "I wouldn't feel nearly so guilty about asking you to do this for me if I knew you could get some personal satisfaction from the trip as well. If there is so little to do here, then this is the ideal time to go—take a few weeks and do the thing right. Visit people. See the Capitol. I'll bet you haven't taken a day off in years."

"That's true," said Robertson. "It sounds like a golden opportunity. When would you want me to leave?"

"Why tomorrow, if you can get ready that quickly. I believe in doing things, not sitting around talking about them. I happen to know that a large group of rental units in Baltimore will be sold this summer. It may be that some of our buildings are in the area being discussed for development. My brother is so busy—he's in shipping—that he has never had time, much less the interest, to note the property management end of our inheritance. I attended to that while I was there. Now he will need help and advice. I wouldn't trust a soul in Baltimore to give him honest guidance."

Robertson looked across the desk, his eyes bright. I'll do it!" he said. "You are entirely correct. I have remained at my post for too many years without a letup. I need to breathe different air. You, sir, have given me the nudge I needed to get me out of my rut. I'm grateful to you for the chance."

Nick nodded. "I'm glad. I'll pay, of course, all your expenses, in addition to commission on sales or rentals. And consultation fees, as well. Keep a record for me, so I'll know what I owe you when you return. And don't feel you have to rush back. Travel a bit. Once our business in Baltimore is settled, you're as free as a bird."

He left the land man making notes for the guidance of his clerk while he was absent. Oren looked ten years younger, his sallow face taking on color for the first tine since Nick had known him.

Bless Alicia! Nick had no idea whether his cousin was possessed of an inordinate amount of intelligence, or simply an intuition that worked overtime. Whatever the situation, she had the capacity to solve problems with incredible ease and many fringe benefits.

He hurried over to the mercantile. There he was forced to wait for a time while Bart helped a middle-aged farmer decide on exactly the correct selections of plow tools for his prospective son-in-law. It seemed like a strange wedding gift to Nick, but on thinking it over he decided that in terms of long-run benefits that might surpass any more usual gift. Continuing income from a farm was the major source of income in the area, surpassing even timber and the mining interests that were growing up.

When Bart was free at last, Nick indicated subtly that he needed something from the nail keg. Bart looked blank for a moment. Then he nodded and opened the storeroom.

"I hate the thought of that being back here, but I can see your point. Until we build a bank that *is* a bank, we haven't any place in town as hard to get into as my storeroom. The present bank's strongroom could be opened with a pair of nail scissors. You going to take it all out?" he asked, his tone hopeful.

Nick took a pack of bills from the leather-wrapped bunch and returned the rest to the keg.

"No. I want to send plenty of money with Oren for expenses. He'll go tomorrow if nothing comes up. He's also going to travel a bit while he's up there. I told him to stay as long as he liked."

"That's just right," said Bart. He secured the inner and outer storeroom doors again. Just leave it to Allie. She scares me, sometimes, when she sees right through a stone wall like that."

The next afternoon, when Oren Robertson boarded the afternoon train bound northward, they all were there to bid him farewell. Ellen Harper volunteered to keep the store, as her school day was finished well before train time. This gave Nick the chance he had been waiting for. He volunteered to drive her home afterward.

Ellen accepted and invited him to meet her grandmother while he had the opportunity. She also asked him to dinner, her grandmother having ordered her to ask him whenever she got the chance.

Nick greatly enjoyed the short drive as well as the company of a young woman who seemed to have something of Alicia's directness and lack of coyness. He liked her, and he didn't try to hide it.

As they pulled up before her house, he turned to look at her. He felt awkward, but he also felt that he owed honesty for honesty.

"You know, Miss Harper, I have been hard put all my life to find someone who can stand comparison with my cousin Alicia. She has spoiled me for vaporings and flutterings of fans. I want you to know that you strike me as eminently suitable to be set beside her in my regard. You are—I hope you won't be offended—a gentleman."

Ellen laughed softly. "Seldom have I been paid such a compliment," she said. "And as I admire your cousin also, I find the comparison flattering. No other women here seem at all congenial, and I have enjoyed knowing her a great deal. Thank you. And don't be nervous. I won't set my cap for you after such a declaration. We gentlemen don't do such things."

Nick laughed heartily. She took his proffered hand and stepped lightly down from the rig onto a block of stone set there for dismounting.

"Come in. Grandmama has been matchmaking busily ever since I first mentioned you. Don't let it bother you. She has had me married off to every eligible gentleman who has visited Moreno for the past five years. Her mind cannot hold the conception of a friendly relationship between the sexes. Partly her Spanish heritage, I suspect."

Nick glanced at her quizzically. Even among the few young ladies he knew in Baltimore who considered themselves bluestockings, such open frankness was lacking. He liked it very much. It had a healthy ring to it that contrasted sharply with the supercharged eroticism that seemed to emanate from such women as Augusta Moran.

They stepped onto the porch, whose wisteria was now losing its bloom. Among the drifts of newly fallen purple blossoms they saw a pair of kittens playing at ambushes around the purring form of their mother.

Ellen stopped to speak to the cat. "This is Nicholas Blasingame, Aurelia. I hope you will like him. I'm certain he will take to you. He strikes me as a sensible person who likes cats."

Nicholas tipped his hat solemnly. "Most happy to meet you, ma'am," he said. Ellen went off into gales of laughter.

On such an auspicious note, they entered the house, stepping into a parlor whose crisp whiteness almost hurt the eyes. Light curtains moved gently in the breeze from the wide windows. The paint of the walls, woodwork, and ceiling was dazzling. A crimson chair with crimson cushions, and a creamy divan whose cushions matched the chair, gave the only spots of color. With the exception of the spines of many books that filled floor-to-ceiling shelves along one wall. As a room, it struck him as one of the most welcoming ones he had ever entered.

"What a wonderful place to sit and read!" he

said.

Ellen nodded. "It is, indeed. Or to talk, if there is anyone worth talking with. Your cousin and her husband come fairly often. Isaiah and son come, too when they aren't having an emergency. Which is too often, I fear."

"Oh, I remember. Alicia said they were related to the founding family. They must be cousins of yours. I find Isaiah and his youngster very congenial. I haven't met anyone I liked much more. Except for the present company, of course."

"Well, you're about to meet Grandmama." A vigorous woman whose black hair showed few streaks of gray entered the room. "This is Nicholas Blasingame, Grandmama. And this is my grandmother, Señora Juana Elizaveta Márquez y Moreno."

She wore an apron that smelled of cooking. Her sleeves were pushed up and a streak of flour marked one wrist. But she greeted him with all the dignity of one used to directing servants in a palace. Age had not bent her straight back, though her face was gently wrinkled as finely as old crepe.

"I am most happy to meet you, Doctor Blasingame." Only a trace of accent hung about her words. "It is seldom that we entertain now. You give us much pleasure. Do seat yourself, while Ellen and I complete the preparations."

Nick groaned. "You couldn't leave me in here to mope, nice as this room is, while you go off into the kitchen and nibble on all the goodies?" he asked. "I am the world's premier kitchen superintendent. Not that I know how to cook, but I am awfully good at tasting to see if things are seasoned correctly. I used

146

to scrape all the cake bowls I could find—but I suspect I'm too late for that."

The dark eyes twinkled. "Indeed, there was a cake bowl. I greatly regret that I did not save it for you. Come, then, if you don't mind. We can become acquainted as we get things ready."

The intangible stiffness that had marked her attitude was gone. Instead of a displaced *grande dame* of old Spain, she was now a lively old lady, eager for a new contact.

As they went along the hall, Ellen smiled at Nick. Her lips moved in a silent "Bravo!" and he knew he had taken the right tack with Señora Moreno.

The kitchen was big. A black iron range dominated it, even so, and from its several ovens and eye plates came steams and scents that made Nick's mouth water.

He perched on a tall stool, much as he had done in Carry-Ann's kitchen, and asked questions, while the Señora poured a sauce carefully into broth, directed Ellen in carving the beef, and kept an eagle eye on the progress of the cake in one of the ovens. Tidbits came his way as if by magic.

By the time everything was ready, he felt he had known Ellen and her grandmother for years. He carried in the tureen of soup to the narrow dining room and set it on a damask cloth of great age and beauty. Heavy silver flanked the china, which looked like Haviland.

The meal was a match for its setting, and the three of them were relaxed and easy with each other. For the first time in a long time, Nick felt entirely at home, even more so than at Alicia's house.

He couldn't analyze why and didn't try. He did enjoy the evening to the fullest, and when he left, it was with a promise to the Señora that he would come again very soon.

CHAPTER TWELVE

With Robertson's departure, things seemed to settle down for a time. Nothing seemed to be happening to trigger Nick's secret schemes, though professionally it was far from true. Word had circulated that Moreno now had a real live Eastern doctor. Even before the new office was ready for business, he was busy working on patients among the bare studs and the sawdust.

That didn't last long, however. Rafe, seeing the need for haste, recruited one of his sons to help him. The partitions were up and painted in jig time. Once the front of the office suite was complete, the facilities for overnight care and Nick's private quarters for temporary use could be finished more slowly.

Looking about, one Monday morning, Nick found himself well pleased with his facilities. Crisp green paint, trimmed with cream, gave a restful air to the place. The bench he had the Hazeltons order for his waiting room was covered with dark green cushions. A plant stand beside the wide front window held a pot of fern that Carry-Ann had insisted he accept. All in all it was a pleasant place in which to wait, even for someone with a bellyache.

For once, nobody had been waiting when he

walked up to his front door. With a sigh, he hung his hat on the curlicued hat rack, went into his office, and put on the white linen coat he wore for consultations. Then he leaned back in the leather chair that Ellen Harper's grandmother had insisted upon giving him and opened the six-month-old medical journal the mail had brought him that week.

The bell, hung from a spring attached to the front door, gave a decisive "Ting!" Nick folded the magazine neatly at his place and opened the office door. Augusta Moran stood in his waiting room, looking around with quizzical eyes.

Before he could greet her, she said, "Well, you seem to have settled in on a permanent basis. And not really a bad job. I could have done a better one—but I wasn't asked." Her big eyes were trying to flirt with him, but he didn't respond.

"If I had known you cared about my personal surroundings, I might have consulted you," Nick said. His voice, he knew, held an edge of hostility. He wasn't enough of a hypocrite to hide it.

"What might I do for you this morning? I hardly think you need my medical skills. I have seldom seen such blooming health."

She laughed. It was an engaging laugh, a rich chuckle with real humor in it. "I have come, Doctor Blasingame, to make an apology. I am not an even-tempered woman. I admit it. I am too Irish ever to be equable.

"I fly off the handle with ease, and I did that with you some weeks ago. It takes a while for my dander to smooth itself down again, which is the reason for my long delay. However, once I calm down enough to see a situation in its true light, I hope I am fair enough to acknowledge myself to be in the wrong." She looked totally sincere, and Nick had to keep reminding himself that this had to be a ploy.

"I regret—I most sincerely regret—my words to you on the occasion when my nephew bothered your cousin's maid."

If Nick hadn't been forewarned by his eavesdropping, he would have believed her completely. She was a consummate actress. Not a false note, not a doubtful expression about the eyes marred the handsome apology. He hoped he could act half as well as she did.

He smiled. "I have never heard a nicer apology. I appreciate your taking the time to seek me out and make it. I haven't, I hope, held it against you. I know how protective women can be of young relatives. Consider yourself entirely absolved of blame."

Her pale violet hat was exactly the shade of her gown. She glanced up at him from beneath the brim in a ravishing manner. He admired the effect, but he found that he was not stirred by her. That was a considerable relief.

"Oh, you mustn't be too easy on me. Do let me do penance! My husband complains that I am never held to account. Let me offer you a dinner at least. Tonight. And bring your cousins!"

Aha! She was offering to "un-ostracize" the Hazeltons! In return for...what?

"I'll be happy to dine with you and your husband," he said. His stomach felt a bit queasy he felt so insincere, but he managed to sound grateful. "However, my cousin has been unwell. I feel that

151

she may not feel up to coming—making that long drive twice. I'll ask her, but please don't be offended if she declines with thanks."

That set her aback. He was certain that Gussie had never had a dinner invitation declined by anyone, even from a death-bed. However, she rallied like a trooper.

"That is a pity. I had looked forward to knowing her and Mr. Hazelton better. Another time, perhaps?"

"Perhaps." He opened the door for her. The violet skirts swirled briefly about his trouser legs as she passed through. The scent of violets wafted about her in the subtlest of waves. He felt sure that this morning she had loaded for bear.

Outside his door, she turned on a gilded heel. "We dine at seven. Boorishly early, I know, by Eastern standards, but we are working folk and must rise early. Is that quite convenient?"

"I'll be there. Yours is the large white house on the hill just west of town, I believe?"

"That's the one." She smiled bewitchingly, billowed her skirts, sending another violet-charged assault against his senses. Then she nodded and moved away toward the milliner's shop.

"Whew!" said Nick, watching her go. Behind him there was a chuckle.

"And now you know," said Doc Pinter, from his office door. "That's the pretty purple glue that has been holding this town stuck to Tom Moran's chariot wheels for so many years."

"How many?" asked Nick with real curiosity. "That is one human being I would never try to guess the age of. She might be sixteen from her complexion and her figure, but she's got to be older than Lilith from her ways. Have you any idea?"

"Six years ago, I'm told, she came here as a bride. She was about seventeen then. So she's still a young woman in years. Old in original sin, I'd say, or I'll eat my second-best boots."

"A dangerous woman," Nick sighed. "I'm to dine there at seven. Do you suppose there will be strychnine in my soup?"

Doc laughed. "That isn't her style, I'm glad to say. She's no Lucrezia Borgia. She's more insidious. Infiltrate and disarm the enemy before he knows he's under attack. That's her way. I've seen her do it a dozen times, and it seldom comes unstuck. Except with Oren. You know, he was actually beginning to criticize some of the things she does—aloud!—before he left for the East?"

Nick nodded. He hadn't confided even in Doc the plan for saving Robertson's life. The fewer who knew, the less chance there was for a slip-up. He was saved from comment by the arrival of a patient. He waved goodbye and went to his work.

Evening found him a bit on edge, however. Alicia had been astonished by the invitation. First she was pleased. Then she was a bit angry, and then she turned off her feelings entirely.

"I'm glad you left us out. I don't need her patronage. She's no lady, believe me. Her approval can't hurt us or help us—not with the people we really respect."

Nick grinned. Alicia's satisfaction at turning down Gussie's invitation was almost counterbalanced by her desire to see inside that sumptuous house on the hill that lorded it over every other home in Moreno.

She did fuss over his clothing for the occasion. She brushed his coat, checked the knot of his cravat; then, standing back, she surveyed him critically.

"I swear, Allie, you'd think you were my mother and I was a girl of sixteen about to attend her first ball. Just make sure there's not a gravy stain on my waistcoat or a rip in my pants. That'll be good enough."

Bart snorted with laughter, catching Allie around the waist. "You've done all you can do unless you want to tag along and send him signals through the window. Let him go, Al. He's got five miles to travel, and he'll be late if you check him out one more time."

She sighed. "All right. But I'll never forgive you, Nick, if you don't remember what kind of china she uses and the silver and crystal. Oh, and her carpets and draperies. I want to know about them. And her servants. Everything. I've coveted that house ever since we've been here."

"I'd choose yours over that one any day of the week," said her cousin, leaning to kiss her cheek. "You get some rest after dinner, Allie. See she does, Bart. I want no more fainting around here."

They stood on the porch to wave goodbye. "You'd think I was going to darkest Africa," he called over his shoulder as he turned into the drive. "Leave a light in the hall for me."

The sun was low, just about to sink behind the trees. The heady evening scent of cool air mingled with forest and flowers, rippling against his face as he touched Lance with the whip. Pale dust whirled up behind the hurrying hooves.

154

Nick, despite teasing Allie as he had done, felt some apprehension beneath his natty cravat. So many things might be decided tonight! Things spoken and unspoken might be of much importance. He must be on his guard every moment.

The lamps had been lit when he arrived. The house beamed down the hill, lights in every window and on the porch. As he moved up the hill, he could see someone standing on the steps. When he pulled up, a shadowy figure slipped from beneath the hedge edging the lawn and took his reins. Nick flipped a coin to the black lad.

A soft, "Thank you, sir," drifted to his ears.

Tom Moran met him at the wicket gate beneath a trellis that breathed roses into the night air. "I'm happy to meet you at last, Doctor Blasingame," he said. "My wife got off on the wrong foot with you, I hear. Too bad. She's fiery, sometimes, but I take it she has it all squared away, now?"

"Quite," said Nick. He crossed the wide veranda with his host to enter double doors set with etched glass.

A uniformed servant took his hat, and Nick had to look twice to recognize one of his patients. He smiled at the man, and the impassivity of the dark face lightened for an instant in return.

Augusta flowed out to meet him. There was a big parlor to the right, a dining room to the left, and a hall full of Gussie in front of him. She wore a rose-colored dress tonight. Her scent again matched the color. In the lamplight her skin was creamy. She had tucked roses into the artless knot of curls cascading down her back.

"Charming," said Nick, bending to take her

hand. "My cousin was devastated that she could not come with me." He saw in her eyes the awareness of just how devastated Alicia had truly been.

En garde! He said to himself as he followed her into the parlor.

Archer Sheley sat on a gold brocade loveseat, flanked by Calvin Andrews and a man Nick had never seen before. Seated with his back to the hallway door was a patrician figure that was immediately recognizable as that of St. John.

The thieves gather, He thought as he smiled and greeted each of them cordially.

Only small talk occupied them as they sat waiting for dinner to be announced. Nick felt he was being lulled into unwariness. He relaxed and contributed his own part to the conversation, letting things ebb and flow. All the while as he listened or spoke, he was studying the men around him, for one was a newcomer Augusta had called David Soames.

This was an odd one. Almost albino fair, he had eyes of a piercing gray. They seemed almost the color of steel in the lamplight. The face had little character, but those eyes boiled with hidden potential.

Nick felt, completely without justification, that he was in the presence of the brain behind the law in Moreno. The Morans, whether they knew it or not, were tools in this man's hands. His very attitude said as much. Nick found himself wondering intensely about the man. Nobody in town had so much as mentioned that name so far. Tomorrow he must ask Doc what he knew.

His thoughts were interrupted by Augusta, as she rose to say, "Dinner is laid, gentlemen. Will you come into the dining room?"

Once they were seated, the small talk was forgotten. Over the soup Tom Moran said, "Doctor, I understand that you have bought the Pinkston farm, beyond your cousins' place. We didn't know anyone was interested in that land, and for that reason we hadn't made an offer. However, a group of people here intend a large-scale purchase in that area. Your place has the only access to the river for the tract we want. Would you consider selling it?"

Oho! thought Nick.

"What a pity," he said. As he spoke, he noted the fine quality of the heavy silver. Baron Gordon, he thought, was the name of the pattern. He must remember that to tell Allie.

"How so?" asked Soames, his steely eyes glinting over his own spoon.

"If I liked the place less well, I might consider offering to sell to you. However, it suits my purposes so nicely, being near to my relatives and also to town, that I really cannot make the offer. You understand, I'm sure."

"Of course," murmured Gussie. She handed him a cut-glass bowl of transparent pickles. "One must suit one's own purposes, of necessity."

The quiet servant appeared at his elbow to take the empty soup plate and replace it with a large plate—Spode, Nick thought. He marked it down in his memory for Alicia's benefit.

"I would be glad to accommodate you, if things were different," he said.

"It would have been quite a handsome offer," said Sheley, holding up his wineglass for a refill. "We have Northern interests involved in this transaction."

"Too bad. But I have already arranged to have the house finished, engaged a man to oversee the work of rebuilding and working the farm, when the time comes. Perhaps you know Rafe Ives? I've chosen him for the purpose," Nick said. He sipped from his wineglass, watching Augusta.

Gussie wrinkled her patrician nose. "Dear Doctor Blasingame! Surely you have not been properly informed! The man is illiterate—and impertinent... really impossible!"

Nick raised an eyebrow. "Indeed? I found him highly intelligent. He absorbed and understood a complicated plan I read to him once. He is fast and skilled. What more could one ask from a laborer?" He cut his excellent beef, tasted the well-cooked vegetables.

"One could ask respect," said Gussie. "That is the one thing that all the servants here lack. They simply do not know their places. Black or white, it makes no difference. They're all opinionated and objectionable."

Nick held his glass to the light. The pale red wine caught the light from the chandelier above him, refracting it through the cut glass. He took another sip.

"My grandmother," he said musingly, "once said to me that she had never met anyone, black or white, servant or master, from whom she could not learn something useful or valuable. If she paid attention to what they said, she learned. Perhaps you have not listened closely enough, my dear Mrs. Moran. But of course my grandmother was a great lady. There are few of her quality anywhere nowadays."

Her great eyes sparkled angrily. He knew she had understood his meaning quite well, knowing that he thought her far less than the lady his grandmother had been—and by inference, that his cousin was.

He had also just rejected her advances and her coquetries, there at her own table and in the presence of her husband, who had not the faintest notion that his wife had been mortally insulted before his eyes. He, in fact, was eating smugly, his face flushed with the wine.

The gauntlet flung beyond recall, Nick was grinning internally. It might take her some time to convince her co-conspirators that he could not be manipulated to their uses. That neither money nor favors would sway him. Yet he knew she would succeed, at last. Then there would be repercussions he was certain.

Looking toward Moran to catch his expression, Nick's glance caught that of Soames. The cold eyes drilled into him speculatively. Nick realized with some surprise that the pale man had caught every nuance of the subtle exchange he and Gussie had just made.

He hoped devoutly that his own expression hadn't betrayed the realization. Nick spoke to Tom, complimenting the wine. Moran nodded, any interest he had previously pretended in Nick's words now lacking. The atmosphere, if nothing else, had conveyed to the shrewd Irishman that something had gone wrong with his plot.

Dessert was carried in—fruit cup, quickly disposed of. The others must have been, by that time, as anxious as he to finish the meal. In a few minutes, they were thanking their hostess, and he was returning with them through the hall to the parlor.

Nick approached Augusta. "I hope you will not be offended, but I truly have to say good night. My days are very full, and I must rest. I like to give my patients the care they deserve."

"Oh?" Her voice was now a bit loud and rather brittle. "I had understood from Mr. St. John that you have not always given that matter a great deal of thought. He says that you were driven out of Baltimore because of malpractice."

Nick found to his surprise that the old memory had lost the power even to make him flinch. "On the contrary, madam, I was driven from Baltimore by a group of men whom I proved had been fattening on the sufferings of the poor. The death of an eighty-seven-year-old man during surgery is an act of God. They seized upon that to make my life so difficult that I had to leave my home." He smiled civilly. "I have learned a great deal since that time. My grandmother's lawyer took my problems much to heart. He gave me good advice that I have not forgotten. He is now, in case you might be interested, the Attorney General of the United States."

The information hit them hard, even through their masks of politeness. If he had been able to pick his time, he could not have had a finer opportunity to convey to them the information.

"He has assured me that he is watching my further career with interest and concern. It gives me a great feeling of confidence."

He turned to the men. "My pleasure, gentlemen. Good night. I trust that I will see you all about

160

town."

As he moved down the flagstone path, he saw that the young horse handler had his rig already at the gate. He handed the youth a coin, and there came to his ears the faintest breath of a whisper.

"Take keer, Doctor. They gwine make trouble for you, for sure."

He grunted his thanks, careful not to let a syllable travel farther than the hedge. Then, clicking his tongue to Lance, he turned toward home.

CHAPTER THIRTEEN

Alicia was waiting up, as he had known she would be. It was still relatively early, and Nick sat in the kitchen with her over a cup of tea. He gave, he thought, a marvelously detailed description of the Moran house—table linens, cutlery, china, glass, and other appointments. He had even noted the carpeting.

When he had emptied that well of information, he saw that she was waiting for something. "Oh, and I insulted Augusta Moran to her bones, perfectly politely and without her husband ever noticing a thing," he said.

He described the exchange to his cousin, and she frowned, a fine line tracking into the space between her pale golden eyebrows. "Was that entirely wise? I thought you'd decided to go along with her for a time. This will put them on notice at once that you are going to fight them."

"I thought about it as I drove to town," Nick answered. "I believe that if we can get this thing out into the open before the election we may stand a chance. Besides, I don't believe they have ever had anyone take the battle to them. They've always chosen the time and the ground, so to speak. This has shaken them up, if I'm not badly mistaken."

He reached to take her hand. "It will, if nothing else, decrease the time during which we will worry about you. You're beginning to show your pregnancy. I think, being the sorts of creatures they are, they would feel that you might offer a golden opportunity to force concessions from Bart and me. And they would be absolutely correct."

She flinched, and he squeezed her fingers lightly. "We can make sure that you—and Bart and I—are guarded, for a short time. But that would get very wearing over a long span of time. If we force their hands, we may see what they're capable of doing and counter it.

"They haven't yet made a try for my money. That's one thing we can watch closely. Oren is out of danger. And as long as we keep close watch on each other, I think we stand a chance of coming out ahead of the game."

Even as he spoke, he was filled with misgivings, which he tried to hide from her perceptive gaze. "Did you ever hear of David Soames? A slender, very pale man about thirty-five or so. He's so pale that he almost looks albino, so you'd be sure to recall him if you had seen him."

She frowned with concentration. "I can't recall seeing anyone like that, but I have heard the name someplace. I can't quite pin it down though." She looked at her husband. "Bart, have you?"

He put down his teacup carefully. "Yes, I have. Not to meet him, but I have heard the name and not in conversation. By chance. When? Hmmm." He put his chin into his hand and thought deeply.

"From Tolliver!" he exclaimed. "Definitely

from Tolliver. I was in the bank, I think. And Tolliver was in Andrews' office, though Andrews wasn't there. He must have been talking to Sheley. His voice went loud for a moment. He said something like, 'David Soames will hear about this, and he won't like it'."

"Sheley shushed him?" asked Nick.

"Must have, for I didn't hear another word from the office. I wouldn't have remembered that at all, if you hadn't said the name. It brought that scene back clearly, once I concentrated."

"Soames, then, isn't a citizen of Moreno?"

"No. Absolutely not. I wonder if he could be that mysterious Northern interest they keep throwing around when they're trying to impress people?"

"He doesn't sound nearly as Northern as I do," said Nick. "But that isn't evidence that he's not. He could be from the northern part of this county, and they'd probably consider him a Northerner."

"I'd say he might be the big money interest though," mused Alicia. Her eyes were very bright. "We've looked into some things around here since we began having trouble with the powers that be. Tolliver's family is land-poor. The Whitfields likewise. Tom Moran handles a lot of money, but he has some big debts. I think he may not own the mine at all. Probably he's a partner in the enterprise and was chosen to manage it. The house on the hill is mortgaged to the hilt. They stay behind with their accounts with the outfits that supply equipment and supplies, too.

"Not local outfits," she added. "I checked it out thoroughly. Companies out of Shreveport and Dallas. I wonder if Soames may not be the principal shareholder in the mine—as well as other things. It isn't always easy to ferret out other people's financial secrets, but I've made a habit of researching credit for the store. That has given me access to some things I might not find out otherwise. People like to talk, too. As I'm a woman, they see no harm in passing along a bit of gossip."

Bart chuckled. Nick patted Alicia's hand. "We'd better watch out, Bart. Pinkerton's may hire her away from us. But I think you're right, Allie. Now what do we do?"

"Wait." She rose and pulled Bart to his feet. "Just go about our business and wait. Keep a close eye on the house at your place. It just occurred to me that they might think of burning it as a means of getting you to sell."

Nick stood, his mind racing. "It makes sense. I'll hire someone to stay there for a while. What about Jimmy? Does his work here keep him busy, or would he be able to camp out in my house for a while?"

"He does odd jobs for me and several others. Hates to be tied down permanently to anything for long. He'd probably like that. It would get him off by himself, and the Indian in him just loves that. Load him up with supplies and set him to guard. He's a good man, just independent as a hog on ice."

Nick laughed at his mental picture of that. "Tomorrow, we'll sound him out. For tonight, it's bedtime. Sleep well, Cousins."

He found, however, that he wasn't able to sleep for a long time. But he thought long and hard, and that sent him to Isaiah Crow's shop as soon as he arrived in Moreno, the next morning.

Isaiah, senior, was taking down his shutters, but he stopped to talk when Nick entered the hop.

Nick looked down at the dark-haired little man. "I think we're going to need someone to keep an eye on my Cousin Alicia. She's expecting. Bart's running for mayor, and the city fathers are like an ant's nest that has been stirred with a stick. I don't know that they would attack us through her, but I don't want to leave it to chance. Who would and could ride shotgun on her for a few weeks?"

Isaiah didn't hesitate. "My son."

"But he's a child!" Nick protested.

"Little Ike has handled guns since he could walk. He's a better shot than the sheriff. He's helped me in this shop, in the business, with every sort of thing you can think of and some you can't. He has a forty-year-old head on that little body. And no one would suspect what he might be doing. She could be tutoring him. He's mighty bright and needs more challenge than Miss Ellen can manage to give him with all the others she has to teach."

Nick's eyes were wide. "That's more than generous. But you have to realize that there's a very real danger here to him as well as to her. Do you think it's wise to risk him? Ellen and my cousin tell me he's a really brilliant boy. I hate to think of putting him into some terrible situation in which he might get hurt."

Isaiah smiled. "We could do it this way. At night she has you and her husband right with her. By day, there in the store, he could sit in her office with her, doing his lessons under her eye. All open and above-board.

"If she had to go someplace alone, he could go

too, books and all. She keeps a gun on her, I know. He can carry my Colt in his book bag. You might fit a shotgun into the buggy and another into some cranny in the store so he could reach it in a hurry."

Isaiah's black eyes were serious. "This town is no place I want him to have to live when he grows up. The thought of losing him freezes my heart, but we've got to fight, if things are going to change. I've known that all along, but until now there's been nobody willing to go along with me, and one man can't do it alone. Particularly when he risks leaving his only child an orphan.

"You're giving us a chance to do what we've been wanting to do. We're with you. I'm not awfully big or terribly strong, but I can shoot, too. When you need me, remember that. And take my son. If we lose him, they will lose far more, I promise you that."

Nick shook the offered hand. "Thank you. I never expected this much. We'll take care of him as well as we can."

So Alicia began spending he days with a quiet child on a stool beside her desk. His dark head was usually bent over his books, but his black eyes missed no motion in the store or out on the street, for that matter. Yet he was so unobtrusive that nobody noticed, except those who knew his secret duty.

Nick returned to his practice and spent a gory morning over an accidental gunshot wound, a broken arm, and a bull goring. The afternoon slacked off, however, and he decided to make a run out to his newly purchased farm. He wanted to make sketches for Rafe to use when he began that project.

Remembering the advice Crow had given him, he stopped by the store and told Bart about the need for a couple of handy but hidden shotguns. Bart went back into the storeroom and came out with three, each in a leather case.

"Put this one in your own rig, Nick. Your hand-gun won't be enough, if you really need it. There's a box of shells in this pocket and another in this one. See, they buckle shut, but you can pull the strap loose mighty fast. Keep it beside your feet, I'd suggest. We can expect the bees to start buzzing pretty soon."

The morning was hot. Spring was well advanced toward summer, and the road was beaten into powdery dust, reddish in the harsh light. The scent of hot pine needles hung between the dark green walls of forest, as he took the track eastward.

The road was empty, as was usual. He gave Lance his head and leaned back in the seat, beneath the hood-like covering of the over-sized buggy. Tipping his hat over his eyes, he relaxed, dropping into a light doze. When Lance slowed to turn into the Hazelton drive, Nick woke and slapped the reins, keeping him headed toward the new place.

Deep dust muffled the sound of the horse's hooves. Nick, urged by an obscure hunch, turned the gelding into a shady patch of woods, some quarter-mile from his own drive, and hitched him loosely within reach of a grass patch. Taking his bearings from the sun, Nick cut across the intervening wood-lot, avoiding the road, and crossed his own fence line at a huge sweet gum tree Bart had pointed out to him on their first visit.

Now he could see glimpses of the house from

the side. A screening of light woods separated him from the lawn, and he eased forward as quietly as his city-bred feet could manage.

From the shelter of a hawthorn thicket, he looked closely at the house and its surroundings. Something had moved, just before he had glanced at the back of the building. He was willing to swear to that.

In the branches above him, a bird rustled the leaves. He froze until it settled down again. Eyes aching from the glare, he studied the outbuildings, the shrubbery, and the young rosebushes running wild in a bed by the house.

Then he heard a definite noise. A door had slammed, without any doubt. He slid backward from the thicket, retracing his steps to the rig as fast as he could. He took the shotgun out of the buggy, removed the case, and filled his pockets with shells. After loading the gun, he turned back the way he had come. Someone was inside his house. If he meant any harm, then a reckoning was on its way.

A terrified bird fled from the hawthorn as he hurried past. He paused, watching again for a moment. Nothing moved outside the house. He felt certain that the intruder was now inside. That slamming door had probably closed behind him as he entered the building.

Nick thrust through the young privet hedge edging the yard on the west and approached the blind side of the kitchen. A huge chimney filled the entire wall there, and he slipped around its corner to move toward the rear door. There he stood, listening, for a long moment.

He heard the tap of heels on uncarpeted flooring, A door opened and closed. The person inside was not trying to hide his presence, that was plain. It sounded for all the world as if a prospective buyer was inspecting the house.

Nick opened the door and stepped inside. "Hello! Is anyone there?" came a call from deeper in the house.

"Yes, there is. Would you please come and talk with me for a bit?" Nick said. He stepped aside so as not to be silhouetted against the light of the door.

Quick taps of heels sounded against the hardwood. A shape appeared in the gloom of the long rear hallway. A short, rather rotund man appeared, wiping his hands on a handkerchief.

"Whoo! What a crop of cobwebs," he said, eyeing Nick with curiosity. "Another buyer, are you? I must warn you I've got the option to buy on this entire tract, including the house here. I was a bit doubtful. The fellow who sold me on it was a tad too slick somehow. You know the kind? You felt there was a con hiding someplace in the deal, even if you couldn't see it with the naked eye."

Nick leaned the shotgun against the wall and held out his hand. "You have to be the gentleman from Ohio," he said. "I am afraid that I'm going to disappoint you. I am Nicholas Blasingame, and I own this acreage. A hundred acres, with the house. I have just bought it from the agent in charge of selling it. Was the man who talked to you an Englishman named St. John?"

The little man stared at him for a long moment before taking his hand and giving it a decisive up-and-down shake. "Tobias Blunt. And from Ohio, right enough. So it was a con? And that slick-talking

170

limey is a scoundrel! Good thing I came on early."

He chuckled. "I took the train as far as that town back yonder." He waved vaguely toward San Pablo. "Then I hired a buggy and horse and came on by myself. I wanted a private look-see, before I talked to any of that man's business associates. I can read deed descriptions like most men read English. I knew I could find the right place, if I could get even the vaguest sort of directions. I came through that little town about five miles back, and a black man in a field told me how to get to the Pinkston place, which was the only name I had for any of the tracts."

He shook his head. "So you're the owner of this part? Good buy!"

"I believe so. I'm a doctor and around here people often pay with produce or livestock and poultry. A doctor really needs to own a farm. And this is all but next door to my only relatives in this part of the world." Nick laughed. "Your man's business associates are in a real bind. They don't want to return your earnest money."

"Hah!" said Blunt, his tone full of enthusiasm. "This the only way to the river from that tract of woods over there?"

Nick nodded. "So I've been told. I haven't been here long enough to walk it out."

"And they don't want to return my money?" Blunt's voice was almost gleeful. "By damn! I've been spoiling for a fight since I left the army. Business is all right, as far as it goes, but I was always one for a good roundhouse battle, if you know what I mean. There's just one drawback. This one will be too easy. My lawyers will have all the fun."

Nick looked the man over. His nut-brown face was beaming with excitement. "If it's just a fight you want," he began. The round face turned up expectantly, like that of a child promised a treat. "We've got a pretty good one coming up. You see, it's this way...." And Nick stood in the dimness of his hallway, telling the tale of the law in Moreno, the problems his cousins had found, even the tale of Carry-Ann's old auntie, to those twinkling brown eyes.

Blunt would nod vigorously, from time to time. "I see! I see!" he interjected often. "A real barrel of rotten apples," he said at last. "And the three of you, with the cabinetmaker, his son, and possibly some frightened black helpers are trying to pry loose this outfit from their ill-gotten influence? Oh, that is choice. It's like a dime novel. I read 'em, you know, just to keep my old fighting blood stirred up. You really would let me in on this?" His tone implied that "this" might be the treat of a lifetime.

Nick smiled. "We've either got to fight or tuck our tails and run."

The little man's face was even ruddier than before. "Never do! Never do! When did you say the election is set for?"

"Next week. They've always stuffed the ballot boxes, so we can't tell how much real good we're going to do at all."

"You need a good campaign manager. Me. I've run elections in Cincinnati for years. You can accomplish exactly what you want to, with an election. This time we've got to get in there and swipe it right from under their noses. Get vote counters from among the solid people. Appoint some poll watchers. You think the honest citizens will vote for our man?"

"They've told us they intend to."

"Good. Then they just may be willing to help a bit. Unobtrusively, of course. Yes, my boy, you need Tobias Blunt. No question about it. I'll start proceedings against the swindlers right here in their hometown at election time, then I'll take over running the campaign." He cocked his head like a robin to look up at Nick.

"A doctor, I know, is too busy to give much time to that sort of thing. Have no fear, Dr. Blasingame. We'll have the enemy on the run before you can say Tobias Blunt!"

CHAPTER FOURTEEN

Blunt's hired horse and buggy had been left in the stable, out of the sun, while he looked over the land. Nick took the time, now, to show the older man over his house, with an eye toward ideas for finishing it out. Then they backed his rig from the stable and went to pick up Nick's.

They sneaked into the Hazelton drive well before dark. Nick found Jimmy in the stables, cleaning out Lance's stall. Knowing that Bart trusted Jimmy completely, he asked the man to tend Blunt's horse. While Jimmy did that, the two others pushed Blunt's rig to the back of the stable, behind a rank of hay bales,

"This gentleman will be visiting us for a while, Jimmy," Nick told him, when they were all done, "We'd rather nobody in town knew he was here."

"Oh. He's the one they was goin' to sell your place to?" asked Jimmy. "They done tracked the wrong bear this time, I can see," Jimmy cackled. "He going to help you all out?"

Nick had underestimated the man's shrewdness. He grinned ruefully. "You're almost ahead of me, Jimmy. But you're on the right track. And while I'm thinking about it, would you be willing to camp out at my place for a couple of weeks? Just so nobody will get the bright idea that they can burn me out and make me turn loose of my land?"

Jimmy cackled again. "I'd do it for nothin'," he said "Like to see anybody sneak up on old Jimmy. I'll take good care of it, Doctor Nick. Don't you worry none. But can you loan me some shells for my old shotgun?"

As it was the same gauge as Nick's, that was easily done. A good part of Nick's shells disappeared into the man's ragged pockets.

"Soon's I finish up Mr. Hazelton's stable and yard I'll hightail it right out to your place," he told Nick. "I'll be there tonight for sure."

Satisfied that he had guarded his back, Nick ushered Blunt up to the house. Bart and Alicia had been waiting supper for their cousin, and both looked a bit worried when they came to meet him. The sight of the stranger startled them a bit, too, but Nick introduced Blunt hastily, and the little man's bluff manner and his shrewd comments soon reassured them. In fact, once an extra plate had been set and the meal had begun Alicia was greatly entertained by Blunt's talk. At last she had to excuse herself in order to go into the kitchen and laugh. When Nick went to help her with serving the dessert, he found her leaning against the wall laughing helplessly.

"Do you remember, Nick?" she gasped. "We had a little brown terrier with eyes just like that. It barked—short, gruff 'whiffs!' exactly the way he does. And his face was round and brown. Oh Nick, I don't know when anything has done me this much good."

Nick felt a grin creep onto his own face. Sure enough, Toby Blunt was the spitting image of the Duke of Clarendon, that long-lost terrier, which Alicia had christened in honor of one of their grandmother's distinguished guests. The real duke, Nick recalled, had not been entirely charmed with the notion, though he had hidden his dismay from small Alicia. She had felt the noble visitor should be highly honored.

Unlike his look-alike, however, Blunt had much more to him than his bark. He threw himself into a whirl of activity the very next day amid universal wonder at the manner in which the Hazeltons had managed to conjure up a house guest from thin air.

His first act was a trip to the telegraph office. There he fired off a ruinously long telegram to the best lawyer in San Pablo, authorizing him to file proceedings against William Exeter St. John, Archer Sheley, *et al.* in the name of T. Blunt Enterprises, Ltd., of Cincinnati, Ohio. This demanded return of certain earnest monies paid against the purchase of real estate feloniously claimed to be salable.

Then the round brown whirlwind moved from the telegraph office to the mercantile, where Nick could see him through the big window (now re-placed), talking furiously with both the Hazeltons. He also stopped every solid-citizen type who went through the door, engaging him or her in earnest conversation.

From his vantage point at his office window, Nick could also see the telegraph agent. The harried man came flying out of the back entry of his office. He made for the bank as if a tiger were after him.

An elderly lady came into the waiting room.

176

Nick greeted her, muffling his chuckles, and took her into the examination room. He knew the conspirators were being told in the most disturbing way possible that the fat was now in the fire.

He could imagine the impassioned rhetoric that must be taking place in Sheley's office. He wondered if Andrews was there, and if the skinny man was a party to the doings of his associate. Nick thought not. Andrews had struck him as the sort who would close his eyes to shady goings-on, not as a willing participant.

The increase in his medical practice was almost irritating that morning. He would have loved to watch, uninterrupted, the drama framed by his front window. Even as it was, he caught glimpses of hurrying figures darting from the bank to the sheriff's office and back. Tom Moran's distinctive figure passed just as Nick was giving last-minute instructions to a young woman, but the death struggles of her two-year-old at the idea of taking the medicine distracted the doctor. He didn't see where Moran went.

There was a feverish feeling to Moreno that morning. Even the least involved of shoppers and business people felt something in the air. At one time or another, everyone who had business in town of any kind at all managed to get to the mercantile.

Blunt collared them as they came. Nick felt sure the coming election would shake Moreno to its roots, for the men who entered the store came out looking angry, thoughtful, and determined.

That night, Blunt refused to "talk shop," as he called it. "You've got your own work to tend to," he told Nick firmly. At that point, Alicia smiled behind her hand and covered it with a ladylike dab at her lips with her napkin. "I've got things in hand already. You just do your doctoring, and I'll see to that election. My God—'scuse me, ma'am—most of those people had never thought there might be something they might do to straighten things out. Now they know!"

Nick had gone on with his doctoring, which was becoming a day and night occupation, as people from outlying areas learned he was in Moreno. The week fled past in a blur of broken bones, new babies, and mine accidents. Never on any of his trips to the mine did he catch a glimpse of Moran or his wife. Hermann Wald reported that the mine owner was making far fewer trips out to the mine than he had been in the habit of making.

On the Saturday before election day, Carry-Ann came to Blasingame as he was eating a late breakfast. "Doctor Nick, can you give me somethin' to loosen up the bowels?" she asked.

"What's the matter, Carry? You or David constipated?"

"Not ezackly. I just needs to know of somethin' that'll keep somebody busy for a couple of days."

Nick's hunch mechanism perked up its ears. "Somebody like the old-timers who always hold the election?" he asked.

Carry's eyes were wide, dark, and innocent. "Why, what makes you ask that? Goodness, looks like nobody can ask you for advice no more. I'll go out and see Old Ma'am. She knows more about growing things that'll do the job, anyways."

Nick knew he should put a stop to whatever plot was cooking. It was his duty as a physician to make sure that nobody was deliberately made ill. But he couldn't make himself take a hand. He trusted Old Ma'am. She wouldn't advise anything that might kill anyone or even make them seriously ill. So he put the affair out of his mind and kept working.

Election Day dawned drizzly. The mud in the streets of Moreno was churned to pudding by nine o'clock. Nick had treated a couple of minor problems and was gazing up the street, watching drops plop into puddles, when a buggy pulled up at his part of the boardwalk.

"Doctor! Will you come with me, please? My husband is really bad sick!"

It was Emily Thrasher, he saw. Her husband had been a deputy of Tolliver's for years. It was her brother-in-law that Alicia had shot in the attempt to rape her. He wondered why she had called on him. Then he had a thought.

"What's the trouble, Mrs. Thrasher?" he asked, taking his hat from the rack and pulling the door shut behind him.

"He's got the runs so bad he can't stand up. And him supposed to help with the election today. I've got some trouble myself, but he's in bad shape. Don't worry about your buggy," she interrupted herself to say as he turned toward the stable. "I'll bring you back. Don't want to waste time hitching you up."

The unhappy Thrasher was sitting on a slop jar with a basin in his lap, busy at both ends. Nick checked him over, as well as he could with so much activity and shook his head.

"It's nothing serious. Just an upset of some sort, something you both ate or drank. But he won't make it to town today, Mrs. Thrasher. Give him this as soon as he can keep anything down. Take a dose, yourself. Send word tomorrow if he's no better, but he should be."

He handed her a bottle of murky stuff from his bag. She put it on the dresser. Without speaking, she took him back to town. It was a silent ride, and Nick spent the time wondering how many of those who were to officiate at today's election had suddenly come down with what Mrs. Thrasher had elegantly called "the runs."

Evidently it was quite a number. Blunt waited beside the office door, a cheerful smile on his red-brown face. "We got most of our counters into the polling place," he chuckled, as Nick led them into the office.

"Your cousin's cook volunteered to take care of most of the regulars. I don't want to know what she did, but I understand there's more upset stomachs in town than you can shake a stick at. You have any idea?" He cocked a quizzical eye at Nick.

Nick shook his head. "She asked me what would 'loose up the bowels'," he said. "I wouldn't tell her, so she applied to a local expert. I'd be willing to bet that little black boys were slipping around to wells and water buckets all night long, pouring in what-ever decoction they came up with. I should have stopped it, I suppose. I had a hunch that was what they were going to do. But I just couldn't make my-self do it. If anybody ever deserved a case of the galloping glums, this crew in Moreno is it."

Blunt laughed aloud. "My thinking exactly. And the black folks, if what I hear is true, have an even bigger stake in straightening this mess out than the whites do. I must say, they've done an effective job."

When Nick went to vote later that morning, Flanders from the bakery was presiding at the polls. As the doctor put his ballot into the locked box, he asked, "Many out and voting?"

Mr. Flanders' rather timid eyes were unusually bright. "You'd think the rain would slow 'em down, but it hasn't. Looks like a record turnout. This time the ballots will be counted right!" he said.

"The polls close at seven?" Nick asked. The man nodded. "And you finish counting after that?" Flanders nodded again.

"Thank you, Mr. Flanders. Let's hope we've all done a good day's work in Moreno today." Nick put his hat on and stepped out into the mizzle of rain.

He trudged over to the mercantile and shook water from his jacket in the shelter of the overhang. Alicia ran to grab him around the waist, whirling him into a waltz step.

"Isn't it fine?" she asked. "All the men are voting. And the votes will have to be counted honestly. Things are going to begin to straighten out as soon as Bart is the mayor."

Nick twirled her toward a waiting customer. "Go tend to business, woman," he said. "I want to talk to Bart."

He managed to get Bart into the back of the store away from listening ears. "Listen, Coz, I am thinking that once the polls are closed, it would be a perfect opportunity for someone to mess things up. Raid the ballot boxes. Stuff in ballots. There are still a couple of the deputies on their feet—not to mention Tolliver. He's weak and woozy, but he's walking. I think we should come back quietly late this afternoon. Hide some men where they can keep an eye on the polling place."

Bart nodded. "I agree. Something else bothers me, too. What if the governor impounds the boxes? Then gets in someone to count the ballots? Someone on their side? Don't forget that the governor is in the Morans' pocket. It has happened before, in San Pablo and several other places that tried to clean up their towns."

Nick rubbed his chin, staring at the wall. "It's time to call in a promise," he said at last. "Grandmother's lawyer promised to keep a close and interested eye on my doings. I wonder what effect a telegram from the Attorney General of the United States of America would have on the governor and Tolliver and company?"

"If nothing else, it should make them cautious," said Bart. "Maybe too cautious to interfere."

"I'll send a telegram of my own right now." Nick put his soggy hat back on and headed for the door.

It turned out not to be that easy. The telegrapher refused to look up from his key when Nick tapped on the counter. When he finally acknowledged Nick's presence, he moved as slowly as was humanly possible.

"I need to send a telegram," Nick said, his tone sharp.

"Ain't sending nothing else this evening," the man said, his voice surly. "Office has been shut down, as of now."

Nick felt a surge of anger. His hand went to his coat pocket, in a gesture he had never made before.

The big Colt came up over the counter. "You are open until five o'clock. You are going to send this telegram right now, or I am going to shatter both your kneecaps so that you will never walk another painless step in your life." He swapped the gun into his left hand and wrote out the message.

The clerk's eyes went to the address. They widened, and his face turned pale as cheese. Without a word, he took the slip of paper in a trembling hand and went to his key.

In less than an hour, the necessary acknowledgment had come through. Nick put the Colt back into his pocket and tossed a silver dollar onto the counter. "Keep the change," he snapped and left the man to his own fears.

At about closing time the rain stopped. Thick clouds still hung overhead, making the sky almost as dark as twilight. Bart came across to Nick's office earlier than they had planned.

"We've got four who will stay and watch with us when the time comes. Alicia's going to Ellen Harper's house. Mr. Crow and young Isaiah are going to keep them company. We're going to pretend we're all on our way home. Then we'll walk back into town and come through from the back street. We can cover the polling place from your office and the bakery. Let's hope we're wrong."

The afternoon passed slowly. Just before the legitimate hour for closing the telegraph office, the skinny fellow on duty there came skittering out of his cubbyhole and all but flew down the street, skidding in the mud at every comer. He passed Nick's window in a blur of motion and hurled himself into the sheriff's office.

Nick had run through his day's quota of patients. He had been about to lock the office and go across the street to the mercantile, but now he thought better of it. He did lock the door from the inside. Then he pulled the long ladder he had had Rafe make for him from its concealing closet, fitted the sections together, and hooked the top of it into two unobtrusive rings he'd put into place beside the overhead scuttle into the attic space.

He found himself, once more, in that stuffy place, trying desperately to make his soundless way to the spot from which he had listened before to such good effect. It turned out to be worth the effort.

There was a low babble of talk below him, obviously in the office. He put his ear to the dusty flooring and listened hard. Sheley was there. Moran. Tolliver, of course, and a couple of his men. And Soames...hmmm.

"This is not any goddam joke!" Tolliver was protesting a bit too loudly. "This is a telegram from the governor himself, and that isn't something that I can afford to just set aside as if it was nothing. We got to talk about things. The game's changed, and there's nothing we can do to make it work the way it used to."

"Then we will change some rules, ourselves." That was the quiet voice Nick remembered from the dinner party. Soames. "While the ballot boxes may not be in your hands, as they always have been, they will be in the polling places until they are counted. At that time they will be taken to the mercantile, I suspect, and locked into that impenetrable vault that they have there. A pity it isn't the bank. We could deal with them at our leisure, if that were true.

"No, they will have to be seized and those responsible for them intimidated so that they will never dare to oppose your interests again. Don't you agree, Mr. Moran?"

"I do, but it's going to be sticky. The governor was pretty hot. He doesn't like to have anybody higher up the ladder on his tail, any more than we do. If we do it quick and clean and everything is set before the ranger the state is sending gets here, I think we can just manage to keep things on an even keel."

"Damn!" That was Sheley's voice. "Why on God's green earth did those idiots in the mercantile have to have a cousin who knows the Attorney General? If we don't do this perfectly, without any questions being asked...smoothly...." His voice dwindled away as if he were questioning the possibility of such effective work.

Nick smiled grimly and wriggled backward to find a spot in which he could stand. Once again, that useful scuttle hole had served him well.

* * * * * * *

They moved through a damp twilight, their boots cautious in the thick mud. Tiptoeing across the boardwalks into the doctor's office and the bakery, they stood at last in darkness, silent, listening to their own breathing. The dim light from the window of the polling place shone faintly in the puddles of the street and gleamed along the wet boards of the walk.

If those counting the ballots spoke, it was so quietly that no one of the men waiting could hear them. Nick leaned against the wall with an ear pressed against the wood. On the other side was the outer office of the jail.

There seemed to be no activity there at all. He leaned forward and touched Blunt on the arm. "Maybe we were wrong," he whispered.

Before the little man could reply, there came the sound of hooves squishing through mud. Nick whipped about to the window and gazed down the street. Six horses were coming up the way, which was now dark except for the lights of the jail and the election hall. The mounted men made no noise, and Nick wondered if more were in the alley behind the election hall.

Blunt, as if reading his mind, slid through the newly opened back door of his offices. Nick knew he would keep anyone in the alley under his gun sight. With a sigh, the doctor nodded to Hermann Wald, who had volunteered to guard the election process in which he was not yet qualified to take part.

They went quietly toward the door and slipped through it. They crept into the jail. The deputy, sure enough, was asleep in one of the cells, as was his habit. Nick closed the door and turned the key, returning it to its hook by the office door.

"That's one we won't have to worry about," he murmured to Wald.

They went into the front office and padlocked the gun case, throwing the key into the spittoon, where it sank without a struggle. Then Nick turned the lamp low, and the two slid onto the boardwalk, hugging the wall as they walked.

The horsemen had pulled up to the hitch rack.

They seemed to be paying no attention to anything except the one among them who was giving orders in a low voice.

In a moment, they all dismounted and moved to the left and right of the door. Then the big man got down and stalked to the door, each boot making a doomful thump as he set it against the wood.

He leaned back, raised his right heel, and brought it against the door lock with shattering force. The door sprang open. The pale face of Mr. Flanders flashed at the window for an instant.

Nick was up and running lightly toward the scene of action. Wald was behind him, and Nick hoped he was being careful with his shotgun. The barrel touched his back from time to time as they hurried through the darkness.

They stopped before they reached the doors of the saloon, which was closed as was mandatory in Moreno on election day. Nick wanted to be certain nobody was lying in wait there. A glance reassured him, and be stepped down into the mud of the cross street beyond.

From behind him be could hear the faint scrape a boot. He knew that Bart and his pair of men were also on the move. He sped across the muddy way to take cover behind the side wall of the tax office, which was used as the election hall.

He heard a babble of frightened voices from inside. The gruff tones of the big man overrode them all.

"We're taking custody of this ballot box, all counted returns, all uncounted returns, by authority of the Sheriff of Moreno County. Anybody objecting can file a complaint with the lawful election official of said county. Anybody object?"

There was no answer. While those outside waited for orders, Nick slipped up behind the end-most of them on his side of the door and clipped him smartly behind the ear with the butt of his Colt. The next in line turned—to face Hermann's big double-barrel. Number three felt a nudge of metal against his spine and prudently froze where he was.

Those across the doorway found themselves facing four shotguns, a Colt, and a Winchester. They thought for a silent moment. Then they dropped their hand-guns to the boardwalk and stood away from the wall, hands up.

Blunt spoke a sharp command; they stepped off the loud wood into the mud and marched toward the jail. They were about to join the deputy, Nick knew.

CHAPTER FIFTEEN

Nick motioned the others back. Something inside him longed to know if he could handle this unusual situation. The years of civilized usage, the decade dedication to healing might have eroded his innate strength, he thought. He had to know.

He stepped onto the boardwalk. His own heels thumped, in turn, toward the door. The big man turned. Tolliver, as he had known it would be. Pale, still, the sheriff was no longer shaky. His hand rose a fraction, bringing his own Colt into alignment with Nick's waistcoat.

"Well, Dr. Blasingame," he said. "You've come to watch me do my duty? I've got to stop this here illegal election. As a good citizen, it's your duty to help me."

Nick smiled. "Duly elected alternates can hold an election. I looked up the code. And they won't count with Moran mathematics. That's what your crew can't stomach. And speaking of stomachs...." Nick found himself laughing wickedly.

"Figured you had something to do with that," the sheriff grunted. "Bein' a doctor, you'd know what."

"I wish now that I had," chuckled Nick. "However, I fear that I can't take credit for it. That's a gift from a selected portion of your constituency, Sheriff, unnamed but potent."

"Well, get out of my way, I'm taking this box to a safe place. I'll put lead through your watch fob if you don't move."

"Go ahead," Nick said agreeably. "Shoot me down, here in front of several of the best citizens of your town. Disregard the telegram from the Attorney General. I'll bet you got one from the governor, too." The man's wince of discomfort told Nick he had guessed correctly.

"You shoot me dead, Mr. Tolliver, and you'll hang. It'll be a small sacrifice for me to make, just to see that your system fails." At that moment, Nick meant every word he said, though later Alicia gave him a tongue-lashing of the first order for his recklessness.

Those in the dimly lit room stood straighter, their faces taking on definition. Flanders stepped forward. He took the Colt from the big man's grasp.

Tolliver's hand drifted downward quite naturally. At the last possible moment, Nick saw his fingers flex to grasp another, smaller gun, whose shape bulged his coat pocket.

Their guns spoke together. The sheriff stiffened for an instant, incredulous eyes glaring. Then he fell at Nick's feet.

Blasingame looked down. His gun fell onto the floor, and he sank to his knees to feel for a heartbeat. He knew there wouldn't be one. The eyes that stared up at him from the floor were dead ones.

Bart's hand touched his shoulder. "You had to do that, Nick. He's been asking to be killed for

190

years, and his cousins, too. I'm just sorry it had to
be you."

Nick swallowed. He reached for his gun, put it
into his pocket very carefully. He rose to his feet,
feeling terribly stiff and old. All his instincts were
crying out against the thing that he had done. That
he shouldn't have been forced to do. Tolliver had
been beaten. He had been surrounded by those who
would have stopped him. Why had he gone for that
gun, knowing that by that action he was forcing his
opponent to kill him?

There came a bustle at the door. Doc appeared,
his hat awry, his coat muddy. "I'd have been back a
long time ago, if I hadn't got mired down. Damn! I
knew there would be fireworks tonight. I just knew
it! Come along with me, Nick. I'll fix you up. You
men tend to things here." The little dentist grasped
Nick firmly and led him up the street toward the office.

Once the lamp was lit, Doc poured a stiff slug
from his trusty bottle and handed it to Nick. "Down
with it!" he ordered. Nick obeyed.

"If I hadn't had to prove to myself that I could
be a damned hero," he burst out, "I could have taken
a couple of men into the place with me, and he'd
have had to give up. He wouldn't have tried to pull
that second gun!"

"Wouldn't he?" asked Pinter.

Blunt bustled into the office and poured another
slug from the handy bottle into a dusty glass that
Doc handed him.

Pinter went on, "I think he'd have tried it if
you'd had the U.S. Cavalry there, Nick. Today put
the handwriting squarely on the wall here in Mo-

reno. The honest people have made it plain they've had enough. Why, Archer Sheley and David Soames took the train north before the election was even over. They saw the handwriting on the wall quicker. I suspect that some big-money boys back East will be mighty unhappy when Soames makes his report."

He refilled his own glass. "Things will be run right here, or at least as right as folks can manage and still be human. And we won't let another crack open up to let in more of the crooks who've been sliding down here to make killings off people who want to buy land."

The old fellow took a long swallow and sighed with satisfaction. "You watch. Once Bart is officially the mayor, Caz Whitfield won't even put his name in for the special election to fill Tolliver's place. He knows things have changed, and he was just damn lucky they didn't change while he was holding the bag, and don't you think he doesn't know it. Tolliver couldn't stand that kind of change. He probably knew you'd kill him. I think he did. Your Colt was in your belt, and he couldn't help seeing it."

Nick sighed raggedly. The liquor was warming his cold insides. Pinter poured another round.

"I think we've got us a first-rate candidate, right here," the dentist said, refilling Blunt's glass. "Mr. Blunt, here, has done a bit of talking with me since he took hold of the election. He's bored blind with Cincinnati, Ohio. He wants to come down here to live. If we can put off the sheriff's election for a few months till he is a legal resident, he'd make a jim-dandy sheriff. I think. What about it, Toby?"

Blunt gazed at Nick over the rim of his glass, his

brown eyes bright. "Ahh!" he said, setting the glass aside. "Yes, I think there's fine scope for plenty of fights here. You still have the Moran interests to cope with. That Soames fellow. I know of him. He's big money from back East, old family, no ethics.

"He won't be easy to get rid of. Particularly if he's the one behind Moran Mines. You'll need a sheriff with no ties to any faction for a while. I think I'd like the job."

Nick could feel a bit of warmth creeping back into him. His stomach had almost stopped rolling. His mind was beginning to work again.

"I think Bart would be more than pleased to schedule the election for you. I know I'd be happy to have you in charge here."

Pinter took the glass from his hand. "Now you and the new mayor, git! You've got a couple of beautiful ladies waiting on pins and needles to see if you'll both come out of this alive. Don't keep them waiting any longer than you have to. And Nick...." He fixed the doctor with a stern and fatherly eye. "If you don't start courting Ellen Harper, I swear to God I'm going to. I know you've been busy, but that's neither here nor there. Get busy, or I'll marry the girl."

Bart appeared at the door in time to hear the last remark. "That's the most sensible advice Nick's ever had," he said "Al's been after him to do that very thing. Now we've got to go show them both that we're still in one piece. Even if all our feelings aren't, quite."

He frowned at Nick. "I know how you feel about hurting people, and how it must feel for you to have to kill one. But you killed a killer. That's all.

Swallow it down, make it stay down, and make it a part of you. You're strong enough to live with it, Nick. I know you. Don't you go worrying Al to death with guilt and depression. With the baby on the way, she doesn't need that!"

Nicholas Blasingame swallowed again. The bile in his throat receded. He buttoned his coat, feeling the unaccustomed bulge of the Colt in his pocket.

This was the new life he had promised himself. He knew that he could, indeed, learn to live with it.

ABOUT THE AUTHOR

The author of sixty-two books, more than forty of them published commercially, **ARDATH MAYHAR** began her career in the early eighties with science fiction novels from Doubleday and TSR. Atheneum published several of her young adult and children's novels. Changing focus, she wrote westerns (as **Frank Cannon**) and mountain man novels (as **John Killdeer**). Four prehistoric Indian books under her own name came out from Berkley. Historical western *High Mountain Winter* was published by Berkley Books under the byline **Frances Hurst**.

Recently she has been working with on-line publishers. *A Road of Stars* was her first original novel to appear in print-on-demand format. Many of her out-of-print titles are now available from e-publishers fictionwise.com and renebooks.com; many of her novels are being published via the Borgo Press imprint of Wildside Press and Amazon.com.

Now in her seventies, Mayhar was widowed in 1999, after forty-one years of marriage, and has four grown sons. The bookshop she ran with her husband for fifteen years was closed after his death. She now works at home, writing short fiction and nonfiction, and doing book doctoring professionally. Her web pages can be found at:

w2.netdot.com/ardathm/
and
http://ofearna.us/books/mayhar.html